CW00417893

If it is profit that a man is after, he should become a merchant, and if he does the job of a bookseller then he should renounce the name of poet. Christ forbid that the business followed by such creatures should furnish a man of spirit with his occupation.

Every year I spend a fortune, and so it would be a fine thing if I followed the example of the gambler who placed a bet of a hundred ducats and then beat his wife for not filling the lamps with the cheapest oil.

So print my letters carefully, on good parchment, and that's the only recompense I want. In this way bit by bit you will be the heir to all my talent may produce.

ARETINO
from a letter dated 22nd June 1537, sent from Venice

Andreas

Oh quante sono incantatrici, oh quanti
Incantator tra noi, che non si sanno!

ARIOSTO

What strange enchanters in our time abound
What strange enchantresses alike are found!

ARIOSTO

HUGO VON HOFMANNSTHAL

Andreas

PUSHKIN PRESS
LONDON

Translated from the German by
Marie D. Hottinger

First published in Germany 1932
First published in this translation 1936

This edition first published in 1998 by
Pushkin Press
22 Park Walk
London SW10 0AQ

British Library Cataloguing in Publication Data:
A catalogue record for this book is available
from the British Library

ISBN 1 901285 01 4

Set in 10½ on 13½ Baskerville
and printed in France by Expressions, Paris
on Rives Classic Laid

Cover illustration: *Palazzo Ducale IV*
Roger de Montebello

CONTENTS

THE WONDERFUL MISTRESS

THE LADY WITH THE SPANIEL

"Upon my soul," thought young Herr Andreas von Ferschengelder on the 17th September 1778, his boatman having unloaded his trunk on the stone steps and pushed off again. "What next? The fellow leaves me standing here, there isn't such a thing as a coach in Venice, that I know, and as for a porter, why should one come this way? It's as desolate a spot as you'd find in a day's journey. You might as well turn a man out of the diligence on the Rossauerlände or under the Weissgärbern at six in the morning when he doesn't know his way about Vienna. I can speak their language—what good is that? They'll do what they like with me all the same. How does one address utter strangers asleep in their beds? Do I knock and say 'My good sir'? He knew he would do nothing of the kind; meanwhile, steps were ringing sharp and clear in the morning stillness on the stone pavement: they took a long time to come near, then a masked man emerged from an alley, caught his cloak about him with both hands, and made straight across the square. Andreas advanced a step and bowed. The man raised his hat, and with it the half-mask that was fixed on the inside. He was a man of trustworthy appearance and, to judge from his movements and manners, belonging to the best society. Andreas was anxious to hurry, he thought it ill-mannered to detain for long a gentleman on his way home at such an hour: he said quickly that he was a foreigner just arrived from Vienna by way of Villach and Gorizia. He felt at once that he need not have mentioned this, fell into confusion, and stood stammering Italian.

The stranger approached with a most civil gesture, saying that he was entirely at Andreas's service. With this movement, his cloak had fallen apart in front, and Andreas could see that the courteous gentleman, under his cloak, had nothing on but his bare shirt, shoes without buckles, and knee-hose hanging down, leaving his calves half bare. He hurriedly begged the stranger not to remain standing in the chilly morning air—he would soon find somebody to direct him to an inn or lodging-house. The man wrapped his cloak tighter about his hips and assured Andreas that he was in no hurry. Andreas was deeply mortified by the thought that the other now knew he had seen his strange *deshabillé*: his silly remark about the chilly

morning air and his embarrassment made him feel
hot all over, so that he too, without thinking, threw
his travelling cloak open, while the Venetian most
obligingly assured him that he was particularly glad
to be of service to a subject of the Queen-Empress
Maria Theresa, the more so as he had already been
on terms of great friendship with several Austrians,
for instance, Baron Reischach, Colonel of the Imperial
Pandours, and Count Esterhazy. These well-known
names, pronounced with such familiarity by the
stranger in front of him, inspired Andreas with the
utmost confidence. It was true that he knew such
great gentlemen by name only, or at most by sight,
for he belonged to the minor, or *bagatelle*, nobility.

When the mask declared that he had what the foreign cavalier needed, and quite close at hand, Andreas
was incapable of declining. To his question, put
casually when they were already on their way, as to
what part of the town they were in, he received the
answer: "San Samuele." And the family to which he
was being taken was that of a patrician, a count,
who happened to have his elder daughter's room to
let, for she had been living away from home for
some time. Meanwhile, they had arrived in a very
narrow lane in front of a very high house, which
looked distinguished enough, but very dilapidated,
for the windows had no glass in them and were all

boarded up. The masked man knocked at the door and called several names; an old woman looked down from a high storey and asked what they wanted, and there was a rapid parley between the two. The Count himself had already gone out, the mask explained to Andreas. He always went out at this early hour to buy what was needed in the kitchen. But the Countess was at home, so they could settle about the room and then send for the luggage which had been left behind.

The bolt on the door was withdrawn, they entered a small courtyard, full of washing out to dry, and mounted a steep flight of stone stairs, with steps hollowed out like dishes with age. Andreas did not like the look of the house, and it seemed odd that the Count should be out so early buying provisions, but the thought that he was being introduced by a friend of the Freiherrs von Reischach and Esterhazy cast a bright light over everything and left no room for despondency.

At the top the staircase abutted on to a fairly large room, with the fireplace at one end and an alcove at the other. At the single window a half-grown girl was sitting on a low chair, while a woman, no longer young but still handsome, was endeavouring to build up the child's beautiful hair into a highly elaborate head dress. When Andreas and his guide entered the

14

room, the child, with a scream, darted into the inner room, showing Andreas a thin face, with dark, beautifully traced eyebrows, while the mask turned to the Countess, whom he addressed as *cousin*, and introduced his young friend and protégé.

There was a short colloquy, the lady named a price for the room, which Andreas agreed to without further discussion. He would have dearly liked to know whether the room looked on to the street or the courtyard, for he felt it would be a dismal prospect to spend his time in Venice in such a room, whether the house was in the town itself or on the outskirts. But he found no moment for his question, the conversation between the other two showed no signs of coming to an end, while the young creature who had vanished swung the door to and fro and cried with spirit that Zorzi must be made to get up at once, for he was lying upstairs in bed with the colic. Then the Countess told the gentlemen just to go up, the boys would soon turn the useless creature out. He would move out at once, and make room for the newcomer's luggage to be taken up. She apologized for not taking the gentlemen up herself, she had her hands full: she had to get Zustina ready to pay lottery visits with her. All the patrons on the list had to be visited that very day in the course of the morning and afternoon.

Andreas would again have liked to know what was the meaning of all this about the patrons and the lottery, but as his guide, with an energetic and approving nod, seemed to take the matter for granted, he found no convenient opportunity for his question, and they followed two half-grown boys, who were clearly twins, up the steep wooden staircase to Signorina Nina's room.

At the door the boys halted, and when a faint groan was heard, looked at each other with their nimble squirrel's eyes and seemed highly pleased. The curtains of the bed were drawn back; on it lay a pale young man. A wooden table by the wall and a chair were covered with dirty brushes and pots of paint, a palette hung on the wall. Opposite to it hung a bright, very pretty mirror, otherwise the place was empty.

"Are you better?" asked the boys.

"Better," groaned the man in the bed.

"So we can take away the stone?"

"Yes, take it away."

"When you have the colic you must lay a stone on your stomach, then you get better," announced one of the boys, while the one nearest to the sick man rolled away a stone which they could hardly have lifted with their full combined strength.

Andreas could hardly bear to see a sick man thus

16

turned out of bed on his account. He stepped to the window and threw wide the half-open shutter: there was water below, sunny ripples were lapping round the brightly painted steps of a very big building opposite, and on a wall a mesh of light-rings was dancing. He leaned out; there was another house, then another, then the lane opened into a big, broad canal lying full in the sunshine. A balcony projected from the corner house, with an oleander on it, its branches swaying in the wind: on the other side cloths and rugs were hanging from airy windows. Opposite, beyond the great waterway, stood a palace with fine stone figures in niches.

He stepped back into the room; the man in the domino had vanished, the young man was standing superintending the boys, who were busy clearing away paint-pots and bundles of dirty brushes from the only table and chair in the room. He was pale and a little unkempt, but well made; there was nothing ill-favoured in his face save for a wry underlip, drawn to one side, which gave him a crafty look.

"Did you notice"—he turned to Andreas—"that he had nothing on under his domino but his shirt? He's like that once a month. I suppose you know what that means? He's a gamester. What else could it mean? You should have seen him yesterday. He had an embroidered coat, a flowered waistcoat, two

watches with trinkets, a snuff-box, rings on every finger, fine silver shoe-buckles. The scoundrel!" He
laughed, but his laughter was not pleasant. "You'll
have a comfortable room here. If you need anything
else, call on me. I can show you a coffee-house close
by where you'll be well served if I introduce you.
You can write your letters there and make appoint-
ments and settle your business—all but what you
generally deal with behind locked doors."

Here he laughed again, and the two boys found
the joke excellent, laughing out loud as they struggled with all their might to drag the heavy stone out
of the room, with a look on their faces of their sister
downstairs.

"If you have any business that needs an honest
man," went on the artist, "I shall be honoured if you
trust me with it. If I am not at hand, see that you get
a Friuli man; they're the only safe messengers. You'll
find some of them on the Rialto and in any of the
big squares. You can tell them by their country costume. They are trusty and close, they remember
names, and can even recognize a mask by his walk
and his shoe-buckles. If you want anything from
over there, ask me. I am the scene-painter there and
can go about the place as I like."

Andreas understood that he was referring to the
grey building opposite, with the brightly coloured

stone steps leading down to the water, which had looked too big for an ordinary house and too mean for a palace.

"I mean the San Samuele theatre. I thought you knew that long ago. As I said, I am the scene-painter, your landlady is one of the attendants, and the old man is a candle-snuffer."

"Who?"

"Count Prampero, who owns this house. Who else should it be? First the daughter was an actress, she got them all in—not the girl you saw—the elder, Nina. She's worthwhile. I'll take you to her this afternoon. The little one is coming out next carnival. The boys run errands. But now I must go and look for your luggage."

Andreas, left alone, threw back the shutters and fixed them. The hasp of one was broken: he made up his mind to have it seen to at once. Then he put all the remaining paint-pots and brushes outside the door and, with a linen rag he found lying under the bed, scoured the paint spots off his table till it shone clean. Then he carried the paint-stained rag out of the room, looked for a corner to hide it in, and discovered a twig broom, with which he swept out his room. When he had finished he put the pretty little mirror straight, drew the bed-curtains, and sat down on the single chair at the foot of the bed, his face towards the window. The kindly breeze came in, stroking his young face with a faint smell of seaweed and sea freshness.

He thought of his parents and of the letter he would have to write to them in the coffee-house. He resolved to write something in this fashion:

My kind and honoured parents,

I have safely arrived in Venice. I have taken a cheerful, very clean and airy room with a noble family who happen to have it to let. The room looks on to the street, but instead of the earth, there is water below, and the people go about in gondolas, or, if they are poor, in great barges rather like the Danube ferry-boats. These boats take the place of porters, so that I shall be very quiet. There is no cracking of whips or shouting.

He thought he would mention too that there were messengers in Venice so clever that they could recognize a mask by his gait and shoe-buckles. That would please his father, who was very eager to collect the peculiarities and oddities of foreign lands and customs. He was in doubt whether to say that he was living quite close to a theatre. In Vienna that had been his dearest wish. Many years ago, when he was ten or twelve years old, he had two friends who lived in the Blaue Freihaus in the Wieden, on the same staircase in that fourth courtyard where the theatre was set up in a shed. He remembered how wonderful it was to be visiting them towards evening, to see the scenery carried out—a canvas with a magic garden, a bit of a tavern inside, the candle-snuffer, the murmur of the crowd, the *mandoletti* sellers.

More poignant than all the rest, the confused hum of the instruments tuning up—to this day it went to his heart to think of it. The floor of the stage was uneven, the curtain too short in places. Jackboots came and went. Between the neck of a bass fiddle and the head of a fiddler a sky-blue shoe, embroidered with tinsel, once appeared. The sky-blue shoe was more wonderful than all the rest. Later a being stood there with this shoe on—it belonged to her, was one with her blue and silver gown: she was a princess, dangers surrounded her, an enchanted wood closed round her, voices sounded from the branches, monkeys came rolling fruit along, from which lovely children sprang, shining. All that was beautiful, but it was not the two-edged sword which had pierced his soul, from the tenderest delight and unutterable longing to tears, awe, and ecstasy, when the blue shoe lay alone beneath the curtain.

He made up his mind not to mention that the theatre was so near, nor even the strange costume of the gentleman who had brought him to the house. He would have had to say that the man was a gambler who had played away everything, down to his shirt, or else go out of his way to conceal that detail. He would not, of course, be able to tell about Esterhazy, and that would have pleased his mother. He was quite willing to mention the rent, two sequins a month—it was not much, considering his means. But what was the good of that, seeing that he had, in a single night, by a single act of folly, lost half his journey money? Never would he be able to confess that to his parents, so what was the good of boasting about his thrift? He was ashamed in his own sight and did not want to think of the three disastrous days in Carinthia, but the face of the rascally servant already stood before him, and, whether he would or no, he had to recall it all minutely and from the very beginning: every day, morning or evening, it would all come back to him.

ONCE MORE he was in the inn *Zum Schwert* in Villach after a hard day's travelling, and was just going up to bed when, on the very staircase, a man stood offering himself as servant or courier. He: he needed nobody, was travelling alone, looked after his horse himself during the day, and the ostler would do so at night. The other would not leave him, went sidling upstairs with him, step by step, as far as his room, then stepped into the doorway, standing square in it, so that Andreas could not shut the door: it was not fitting for a young gentleman of quality to travel without a servant: it would look paltry down in Italy, they were infernally nice on that point. And how he had done little else all his life but ride abroad with young gentlemen—his last was Freiherr Edmund von Petzenstein, and before that the canon, Count Lodron—Herr von Ferschengelder must know them. How he had ridden ahead as travelling courier, ordered everything, arranged everything, till the count was speechless with amazement, "he had never travelled so cheap," and their quarters were of the best. How he spoke Flemish and Romansch and Italian, of course, as fluently as you please, and knew all about the money, and the tricks of inn-keepers and postilions—nobody could beat him there; all they could say was: "There's no coming at your gentleman. He's in safe hands." And how he knew all about buying a horse, so that he could get the better of any horse-dealer, even the Hungarians, and they were the best, let alone the Germans or Walloons. And as for personal service, he was valet and barber and perruquier, coachman and huntsman, beater and loader, knew all about hounds and guns, correspondence, casting accounts, reading aloud, writing *billets* in all languages, and could serve as interpreter or, as the Turks say, dragoman. It was a marvel that a man like him was free, and indeed the Freiherr von Petzenstein had wanted his brother to have him *à tout prix*, but he had taken it into his head to be servant to Herr von Ferschengelder—not for the wages—that was of no matter to him. But it would just suit him to be of assistance to a young gentleman making his first tour, and to win his affection and esteem. It was confidence he had set his heart on, that was the reward that a servant like him looked for. What he wanted was friendship and trust, not money. That was why he had not been able to hold out in the Imperial Cavalry, where there was nothing but tale-bearing and the stick—no trust. Here he passed his tongue over his moist, thick lip like a cat.

At this point Andreas stopped him, saying that he thanked him for his obliging offer, but did not mean to hire a servant then. Later, perhaps, in Venice, a paid lackey—and here he made as if to shut the door, but the last sentence was already too much; that little flourish—for he had never thought of hiring a footman in Venice—took its revenge. For now the other, feeling in the uncertainty of his tone who was the real master in the dispute, blocked the door with his foot, and Andreas could never make out later how it was that the ruffian forthwith, as if the matter were already settled between them, spoke of

his mount—there would be a bargain that day the
like of which would never come again. That very
night a horse-dealer was passing that way: he knew
him from his time with the canon—not a Turk, for
once. The man had a little Hungarian horse to sell
which might have been made for him. Once he got
that between his legs, he would make a high-stepper
of it inside of a week. The bay was priced, he
thought, at ninety *gulden* for any one else, but at sev-
enty for him. That was because of the big horse-deal
he had put through for the canon, but he would
have to clinch the bargain that very day before midnight, for the dealer got up early. So please would
his honour give him the money at once, out of his
waist-belt, or should he go down and bring up his
portmanteau or his saddle, for he would have his
capital sewn up there—a gentleman like him would
only carry the bare necessary on him?

When the wretch spoke of money, his face took on
a loathsome look; under the impudent, dirty blue
eyes little wrinkles twitched like ripples on water. He
came close up to Andreas, and over the protruding,
moist, thick lips floated a smell of brandy. Then
Andreas pushed him out over the threshold, and the
fellow, feeling the young man's strength, said no
more. But again Andreas said a word too much, for
he felt too rough handling the intruder thus ungently.

Count Lodron would never have been so rough, he thought, or laid his hands on him. So he added, partly by way of dismissal, that he was too tired today, they could think about it next morning. In any case, nothing had been settled between them for the moment.

He meant to leave without further discussion next morning as early as possible. But in that way he merely twisted the rope for his own neck, for in the morning, before it was even light and Andreas was awake, there was the fellow already standing at the door, saying that he had already saved five *gulden* cash for his honour, had bought the horse—a beauty—it was standing down in the courtyard, and every *gulden* Herr von Ferschengelder should lose when he got rid of the horse in Venice was to be struck off his own wages.

Andreas, looking out of the window, drunk with sleep, saw a lean but spirited little horse standing down in the courtyard. Then the conceit seized him that it would be, after all, a very different matter to ride into towns and inns with a servant riding behind him. He could lose nothing on the horse—it was certainly a bargain. The bull-necked, freckled fellow looked burly and sharp-witted, nothing worse, and if Freiherr von Petzenstein and Count Lodron had had him in their service, there must be something in him. For in his parents' house in the Spiegelgasse, Andreas had breathed in with the air of Vienna a boundless awe of persons for rank, and what happened in that higher world was gospel.

So there was Andreas with his servant riding behind him, carrying his portmanteau, before he even knew or wanted it. The first day everything went well, and yet it seemed ugly and dreary to Andreas as it passed, and he would have preferred not to live through it again. But it was no use wishing.

Andreas had intended to ride to Spittal, and then through the Tyrol, but the servant talked him into turning left and staying in the province of Carinthia. The roads, he declared, were much better there, and the inns without their like, and life far merrier than among those blockheads in the Tyrol. The Carinthian maids and millers' daughters had a way with them, and the roundest, firmest bosoms in all Germany— there was a saying about them, and many a song. Didn't Herr von Ferschengelder know that?

Andreas made no answer; he shuddered hot and cold beside the fellow, who was not so much older than he—five years at most. If he had known that Andreas had never seen, let alone touched, a woman without her clothes, some shameless jeer would have been forthcoming, or talk such as Andreas could not even imagine, but then he would have torn him from his horse and set upon him in a fury—he felt it, and the blood throbbed in his eyes.

They rode in silence through a wide valley; it was a rainy day, grassy hill-slopes rose right and left, here and there a farm, a hayrick, and woods high above on which the clouds lay sluggishly. After dinner Gotthilff grew talkative—had the young master taken a look at the landlady? She was nothing much now, but in '69—that was nine years ago, when he was sixteen years old—he had had that woman every night for a month. Then it had been well worthwhile. She had had black hair down to below the hollows of her knees. And he urged on his little horse and rode quite close to Andreas, till Andreas had to warn him not to ride him foul—his chestnut could not stand it. In the end she got something to remember him by, it had served her right. At the time he had been with a countess's waiting-woman, as pretty as a picture, and the landlady had smelt a rat and gone quite thin with jealousy, and as hollow-eyed as a sick dog. At that time he had been courier to Count Porzia—it was his first place, and a fine surprise it had been for all Carinthia that the Count had made him his huntsman at sixteen, and confidential servant into the bargain.

But the Count knew very well what he was doing, and whom he could trust, and he had good need of

somebody who could keep his mouth shut, for the
Count had more love-affairs than teeth in his head,
and many a married man had sworn to kill him,
gentlemen and farmers too, and millers and huntsmen. Just then the Count was carrying on with the
young Pomberg Countess—she was like a vixen in
love, but she was no more in love with the Count
than her maid was in love with him, Gotthilff. And
when her husband had had the shoot in Pomberg
the Countess had stolen to Count Porzia's stand—
crawling along on all fours, and meanwhile the
Count had given him his piece and told him to
shoot for him, so that nobody should notice, and
nobody had noticed, for he was just as good a shot
as the Count. And once, he had brought down a
fine deer at somewhere about forty paces, through
undergrowth: he had caught a glimpse of its shoulder in the dusk. Then the animal had collapsed
under his fire, but at the same time a woeful cry had
come out of the thicket—it sounded like a woman,
but directly afterwards all was still again, as though
the wounded woman had held her mouth shut with
her own hand. Of course, he could not leave his
stand then, but the next day he had paid a visit to
the landlady and had found her in bed with wound-
fever. And he had been smart enough to find out
that she had been driven into the wood by jealousy,

because she thought the waiting-woman was out with him and that she would find them in the undergrowth together. He had split his sides with laughing, to think she had got something to remember him by, and from his own hand, and all the same couldn't upbraid him with it, but had to listen to his jeers, and sharp ones too, and hold her tongue to everybody, and lie herself out of it by saying that she had fallen on the scythe and cut herself over the knee.

Andreas pressed on, the other too; his face, close behind Andreas's, was red with wild, shameless lust, like a fox in rut. Andreas asked whether the Countess was still alive. Oh, she? She had made many a man happy, and still looked no more than twenty-five, and for that matter the ladies in the big houses here, if you only knew how to take them, where a country-woman would only give her finger, would give their whole hand, and all the rest with it. Now he was riding close behind Andreas, but Andreas paid no heed. The wretch was as loathsome to him as a spider, yet he was but twenty-two, and his young blood was afire with the talk, and his thoughts were wandering elsewhere. He might, he thought, be arriving himself at Pomberg Castle that evening, an expected guest along with other guests. It is evening—the shoot is over, he was the best shot: wherever he fired something fell. The lovely Countess was at his side as he fired, her eyes playing with him as he with the life of the wild creatures. Now they are alone—an utterly solitary room, he alone with the Countess, walls a fathom thick, in deathly silence. He is appalled to find her a woman, no longer a Countess and young cavalier—nothing gallant nor fine about it all, nor beautiful either, but a frenzy, a murdering in the dark. The ruffian is beside him, emptying his gun on a woman who has crept to him in her nightdress. He has started back to the dining-room with the Countess, his thoughts dragging him back to the lighthearted decency there—then he felt that he had pulled up, and at the same moment his servant's nag stumbled. The man cursed and swore, as if the rider ahead were not his master, but someone he had fed swine with all his life. Andreas let it pass. He felt a great lassitude, the broad valley looked endless under the sagging clouds. He wished it were all over, that he were older and had children of his own, and that it was his son who was riding to Venice, but a different man from him, a fine fellow, and that the world was clean and kindly, like Sunday morning with the bells ringing.

The next day the road mounted. The valley narrowed, steeper slopes, from time to time a church on a height, far below them rushing water. The clouds were on the move, now and then a shaft of sunlight shot down to the river, where, among willows and hazels, the stones gleamed livid, the water green. Then gloom again, and gentle rain. A hundred paces further the new-bought horse fell lame, its eyes were glazed, its head looked aged, the whole beast changed. Gotthilff broke out that it was small wonder, when the horses were tired in the legs and a man pulled up his beast on the road in the twilight, without a by your leave, so that the man behind could not help stumbling. He had never seen such manners; in the cavalry he would have been put in irons for it.

Again Andreas let it pass; the fellow knows something about horses, he said to himself, he thinks he's responsible for the horse, that's what maddens him. But he wouldn't have taken that tone with the Freiherr von Petzenstein. It serves me right. There's something about a great gentleman that a lackey respects. There's nothing of the kind about me: if I tried to put it on it wouldn't suit me. I'll take him along with me till Saturday, then I shall sell the horse, though I lose half the money, and pay him off; a man like that will find ten places for one he loses, but he needs a firmer hand than mine.

Soon they were riding at a foot-pace; the horse's head looked thin and jaded, and Gotthilff's face bloated and furious. He pointed to a big farm in front of them, to the side of the road—there they would stop: "I'm not going to ride a dead-lame beast a step further."

THE HOMESTEAD was more than substantial. A square of stone wall ran round the whole, with a stout turret at each corner; the gate was framed in stone, with a coat of arms above. Andreas thought it must be a gentleman's house. They dismounted, Gotthilff took the two horses—he had to pull rather than lead the bay through the gate. The courtyard was empty save for a fine big cock on a dunghill, surrounded by hens; on the other side a little stream of water flowed from the fountain, and made its way out under the wall, among nettles and briars: ducklings were swimming on it. There was a tiny chapel, with flowers against it growing on trellises, and all this was within the wall. The path leading across the farmyard was flagged, the horses' hoofs clattered on it. The path led straight through the house under a huge vaulted archway. The stables must be behind the house.

Then farm-hands appeared, with a young maid, followed by the farmer himself, a tall man, not much over forty, and slim and handsome. A stable was allotted to the strangers, Andreas was shown to a pleasant room in the upper storey. Everything gave the impression of a well-to-do house where nobody is put out by the arrival of even unexpected guests. The farmer glanced at the little bay, went up and looked at the horse between its forelegs, but said nothing. The two strangers were bidden to table at once.

The room was massively arched, on the wall a huge crucifix, in one corner the table, with the meal already standing on it. The men and maids sat spoon in hand, at the head of the table the farmer's wife, a big woman with an open face, but not so handsome and cheerful as her husband; beside her the daughter, as tall as her mother, yet still a child, with her mother's regular features, though all lighting up with pleasure at every breath, like her father's.

With the memory of the meal that followed Andreas struggled as with some mouthful of horror that he must get down his throat, whether he would or no. The farmer and his family so kind, so trustful, everybody so frank and mannerly, so unsuspicious, the grace pleasantly spoken by the farmer, the wife attentive to her guest, as if he had been her son, the men and maids neither bold nor bashful, and between master and man the same frank kindliness. But there sat Gotthilff, like a bull in the young corn, insolent and patronizing with his master, lewd and overbearing with the servants, guzzling, showing off, bragging. It gripped Andreas's throat to see the lengths to which the ruffian could go, and still laugh: it pierced him tenfold to see how unabashed he was in his shameless silliness. He felt as though his soul enfolded every one of the servants, and the farmer and his wife as well. The farmer's brow seemed to grow so still, and his wife's face stern and hard—he longed to get up and give Gotthilff what he deserved, beating his face with his fists till he should collapse, bleeding, and have to be carried out feet foremost.

At last the meal came to an end, grace was said—at any rate he ordered the ruffian at once to the stable to see to the sick horse, and in so peremptory a tone that the man looked at him amazed, and, although with a grimace and a scowl, immediately betook himself out of the room. Andreas went upstairs—thought he would go and have a look at the horse—thought better of it, to avoid seeing Gotthilff—was standing in the archway—a door was ajar in it—the girl Romana appeared and asked him where he was going. He: he didn't know how to kill the time; besides, he ought to have a look at the horse so as to find out whether they would be able to leave the next day. She: do you have to kill it? It passes quickly enough for me. It often frightens me.

Had he been in the village? The church was really beautiful; she would show it to him. Then, when they came back, he could have a look at the horse; his man had been poulticing it with fresh cow-dung.

Then they went out at the back of the farmyard; between the byre and the wall was a path, and beside one of the corner turrets a little gate led into the open. On the narrow footpath up through the fields they talked freely; she asked whether his parents were still alive—whether he had brothers and sisters. She was sorry for him there, being so much alone. She had two brothers; there would have been nine of them if six had not died. They were all little innocents in Paradise. Her brothers were woodcutting up in the convent wood. It was a merry life in the woodcutters' hut; they had a maid with them too. She was to go herself next year—her parents had promised.

Meanwhile they had reached the village. The church stood off the road, they entered, whispered. Romana showed him everything: a shrine with a knuckle of St. Radegunda in a gold casket, the pulpit with chubby-cheeked angels blowing silver trumpets, her seat, and her parents' and brothers', in the front pew, and, at the side of the pew, a metal shield, which bore the inscription *Prerogative of the Finazzers*. Then he knew her name.

They left the church on the other side and went into the churchyard. Romana moved about the graves as if she were at home. She led Andreas to a grave with a number of crosses on it, one behind the other. "Here lie my little sisters and brothers, God keep their souls," she said, and bent to pull up a weed or two from among the lovely flowers. Then she took a little holy-water stoup from the foremost cross. "I must fill it again, the birds are always perching here and upsetting it." Meanwhile Andreas was reading the names; there were the innocent boys Egidius, Achaz, and Romuald Finazzer, the innocent girl Sabina, and the innocent twins Mansuet and Bibiana. Andreas was moved with inward awe to think they had had to depart so young—not one had been on earth for even so much as a year, and one had lived only one summer and one autumn. He thought of the warm-blooded, jovial face of the father, and realized why the mother's regular features was harder and paler. Then Romana came back from the church with the holy water in her hand, reverently careful not to spill a drop. Thus gravely intent she was indeed a child; but unconsciously, and in her beauty, grace, and stature, already a woman. "There's none but my kin hereabout," she said, and looked with shining eyes over the graves. She felt happy here, as she felt happy sitting between her father and mother at table, and lifting her spoon to her shapely mouth. She followed Andreas's eyes: her look could be as steady as an animal's, and, as it were, carry the look of another as it wandered.

Built into the church wall behind the Finazzer graves there was a big, reddish tombstone, with the figure of a knight on it, armed *cap-à-pie*, helm in arm, a little dog at his feet, with its paws touching a scutcheon. She showed him the little dog, the squirrel with the crown between its paws, and crowned itself, as a crest.

"That is our ancestor," said Romana. "He was a knight, and came over from the Italian Tyrol."

"So you are gentry, and the arms painted on the sundial are yours?" said Andreas.

"Why, yes," said Romana with a nod. "It is all painted in the book at home that is called *The Roll of Carinthian Nobles*. It goes back to the time of Emperor Maximilian I. I can show it to you if you like."

At home she showed him the book, and took a real child's delight in all the handsome crests. The wings, leaping bucks, eagles, cocks, and a green man—nothing escaped her, but her own crest was the finest, the little squirrel with the crown in its paws—it was not the most beautiful, but she loved it best. She turned over the pages for him, leaving him time to look. "Look! Look!" she cried at each page. "That fish looks as fierce as a fresh-caught trout— what a hideous buck!"

Then she fetched another book: the pains of hell were pictured there, the tortures of the damned arranged under the seven deadly sins, all engraved on copper. She explained the pictures to Andreas, and how each punishment arose exactly from its sin. She knew everything and said everything, frankly and artlessly, and Andreas felt as if he were looking into a crystal holding the whole world, but it was innocent and pure.

They were sitting side by side in the big room on the window-seat running round the embrasure; then Romana stopped and listened, as if she could hear through the wall. "The goats are home. Come and look at them." She took Andreas by the hand, the goatherd put down the milking-pail, the goats crowded round it, trying to get their swollen udders in. There were fifty of them; the goat-boy was quite beleaguered. Romana knew them all. She pointed out the most vicious and the quietest, the one with the longest hair and the best milker. The goats knew her too, and came running to her. Over by the wall there was a grassy spot. Hardly had the girl lain nimbly down when a goat was standing over her to let her drink, and struggled to stay there till she had

sucked, but Romana sprang behind a barrow, drawing Andreas by the hand. The goat could not find
the way, and bleated piteously after her.

Meanwhile Romana and Andreas climbed the
spiral staircase of the turret looking towards the
mountains. At its top there was a little round room,
where an eagle was huddled on a perch. Across its
stony face and lifeless eyes a light flashed, it raised its
wings in faint joy, and hopped aside. Romana sat
down beside it and laid her hand on its neck. Her
grandfather had brought it home, she said, when it
was barely fledged. For as to clearing out eyries, he
had not his like for that. He never did much else,
but often he would ride far away, climb about, track
down the eyrie somewhere in the rocks, rouse the
countryfolk, the cowherds, and huntsmen, and make
them tie the longest ladders together or let him
down on ropes almost out of sight. He was good at
that, and at marrying handsome women. He had
married four of them, and as each died took a still
handsomer one, and every time a kinswoman, for he
said there was nothing like Finazzer blood. When he
had caught the eagle he was already fifty-four, and
had hung for nine hours at the end of four church
ladders over a most frightful precipice, but directly
afterwards, he had gone courting his handsomest
wife. She was a young cousin's widow, and had

never looked at any one but him, was almost glad when her husband was killed—by a runaway ox, that was—though she had a little girl by him and was far gone with child at the time. And so her father and mother were half-sister and half-brother, her mother a year older than her father, and that was why they were so dear to each other, because they were of one blood and had been brought up together. When her father rode away to Spittal or over into the Tyrol to buy cattle, even if it were only for a night or two, her mother could hardly let him go; she cried every single time, clung to him, kissed his mouth and hands, and could not stop waving, and looking after him, and calling blessings on him. And that was how she was going to live with her husband—she would not have it any other way.

Meanwhile they had crossed the yard. Beside the gate, inside the wall, there was a wooden bench; she drew him towards it and told him to sit down beside her. Andreas marvelled how the girl told him every-thing, as frankly as if he had been her brother. Meanwhile evening had drawn in—on the one hand, the clouds had sunk down over the mountains, on the other there was a piercing clearness and purity, with a few golden clouds scattered over the sky, the whole sky in movement, the puddle with the quacking ducks a spray of fire and gold, the ivy on the chapel wall like emerald; a tit or robin glided out of the green gloom, and wheeled with a sweet sound in the shimmering air. Romana's lips were loveliest of all: they were shining, transparent crimson, and her eager, innocent talk flowed between them like fiery air carrying her soul, while from the brown eyes came a flash at every word.

Suddenly, over in the house, Andreas saw her mother standing in an embrasure in the upper storey and looking down at them. He he pointed her out to Romana. Through the leaded window the woman's face looked sad and stern; he thought they ought to get up and go into the house, her mother might need her, or she did not like them sitting there together. Romana merely gave a frank and happy nod, drew him by the hand. He was to stay where he was. The mother nodded back and went away. Andreas could hardly understand this; the only attitude he knew towards parents and elders was constraint and fear: he could not imagine that the mother could find such freedom anything but displeasing, even though she might not say so. He did not sit down again, but said he must have a look at the horse.

When they entered the stable the young maid was crouching by the fire, her hair hanging in wisps over her flushed face, the servant more on than beside her. She seemed to be brewing something in an iron pot.

"Shall I go for more saltpetre, Mr Sergeant?" asked the slut, tittering as if it were some great secret. When the ruffian saw Andreas with Romana behind him he scrambled into a more decent posture. Andreas ordered him to take the portmanteau, which was still lying in the straw, up to his room, and the valise, too.

"All in good time," said Gotthilff. "I've got to get finished here first. That's a draught to make a sick horse sound and a sound dog sick." As he said this he turned to Andreas with a most insolent look.

"What's the matter with the horse?" said Andreas, and stepped towards the stall, but he halted before the second step because he realised that he knew nothing about it, and the bay looked the picture of misery.

"What should be the matter? Tomorrow it will be all right. Then off we go," replied the fellow, and turned back to the fire.

Andreas took the portmanteau, pretending he had forgotten his order to the servant. He pondered whether he was pretending to himself, to the fellow, or to Romana. She followed him upstairs. He left the door open behind him, threw the portmanteau down; the girl came in carrying the valise, and laid it down.

"That's my grandmother's bed. She bore her children in it. Look how beautifully it is painted, but my mother and father's bed is much grander, and still bigger. It has St James and St Stephen painted at the head, and lovely wreaths of flowers at the foot. This is shorter, because my grandmother was not over big. I don't know if it will be long enough for you. It's so short. We're of a height. Let's try whether we can sleep in it full length. It's no sleep at all to sleep all doubled up. Mine is long and broad. There's room enough for two in it."

Nimbly she swung her big, light limbs on to the bed and lay full length in it, the tips of her toes touching a moulding at the foot of the bed. Andreas was bending over her. She lay as joyous and innocent under him as she had lain under the goat. Andreas looked at her half-open mouth, she stretched out her arms, and drew him gently to her, so that his lips touched hers. He straightened himself—it flashed through him that this was the first kiss of his life. She let him go, then gently drew him to her again, and gave him another kiss, and then, in the same way, a third and fourth. The door swung in the wind—Andreas felt that somebody had looked in. He went to the door and out into the passage—it was empty. Romana followed close behind, he went downstairs without a word, and she followed him, quite buoyant and free.

Downstairs, her father was standing telling the

foreman how to bring in the part of the aftergrowth which had dried first. She ran confidingly to him and leaned against him. Standing beside the great child, the handsome man might have been her betrothed.

Andreas went towards the stable as if he had important business there. The servant came hastily out of the gloom, nearly ran into him, cried "Hallo there!" as though he had not recognized his master, and at once talk spurted from his moist mouth. The maid—that was a fine girl for you, she was busy helping him to cure the horse. She didn't come from here either: she came from the valley, and could do what she liked with the farmer folk. But the master needed no telling; he knew pretty well what he was about: he had got a young and pretty one. Well, well, that was the way in Carinthia—that was life! For by the time they were fifteen every maid had had her man, and the farmer's daughter was just as willing to leave her door unbolted as the dairymaid, one today, another tomorrow, so that everybody got his chance. There was a fire in Andreas's breast which leapt to his throat, but not a word left his mouth. He longed to strike the fellow across the mouth—why did he not do so? The other felt it, and recoiled half a pace. But Andreas's mind was elsewhere. His eyeballs quivered. He saw Romana sitting in the dark on her virgin bed, in her nightgown, her feet drawn up under her, watching the door. She had shown him her door and the empty room beside it, and it all rolled past his eyes like mountain mist. He did not want to pursue the thought—strove to turn away from it. Without more ado he turned his back on the wretch, who had won the day again.

At the evening meal Andreas felt as he had never felt in his life: everything had fallen apart—the shadows and the light, the faces and the hands. The farmer stretched out his hand towards him for the cider jug. Andreas was startled to the depths of his being, as if the hand of doom were groping for the veins of his heart. At the other end of the table the maid was cackling her "Mr Sergeant!" "Who should that be?" demanded Andreas angrily. His voice sounded so strange, like a dreamer talking in his sleep. From far away the servant stared at him, white and unkempt—sullen.

Later, Andreas was alone in his room. He was standing by the table fidgeting with his portmanteau—there was a tinder-box, but he needed no candle: the moon shone bright through the window, casting black shadows. He was listening to the noises in the house, he had taken off his riding-boots—he did not know what he was waiting for. And yet he knew, and suddenly found himself standing out in the passage in front of a bedroom door. He held his breath. Two people, lying together in bed, were talking in a low, confiding tone. His senses quickened, he could hear the farmer's wife plaiting her hair as she spoke, and the house-dog moving about in the yard eating something. "Who can be feeding the dog at this time of night?" something in him wondered, and at the same time it seemed to him as if he must return to his boyhood, when he still slept in the little room next to his parents and overheard them talking in the evening through the wardrobe in the wall. Even now he did not want to eavesdrop, yet he heard all the same, but through what he heard he could hear his parents talking—they were certainly older than the farmer and his wife, yet not much—ten years maybe. "Is that so much?" he thought; "are they so much nearer death—worn out? For every word they say could be left unspoken; one speaks, the other replies, and real life passes by. But those two in there are as confiding and warm-hearted as a newly married couple."

Suddenly he started as if an icy drop had fallen straight on to his heart. They were speaking of him and the girl, but even that was harmless. Whatever the child might do, said the wife, she let her have her way, because the girl would never carry on behind her back. She was too straightforward; she got that from him, for he had always been a fiery friend and a happy-natured man, and now, by God's goodness, the girl had grown like that too. No, said the husband, she got that from her, because she was her mother's child, and so there could be nothing deceitful or underhand in her.—But now here she was, nothing but an old woman, with a daughter already running after a strange man, and the time would soon come when he would be ashamed to treat her like a lover.—No, God save him, she was always the same to him—nay more, always dearer, and these eighteen years he had not rued it for one hour. No, nor had she, not for an hour. He was the only thing she cared for; and, his pleasant voice replied, he cared only for her and the children; they were one with her, those that were left, and the others too. And that old couple the Schwarzbach had swept away in the April floods might be counted happy. They had floated away on a bed together, holding each other's hands, and the river had carried them down into the mill-race, and her white hair had shone like silver under the willows. And that was what God gave to His chosen. That was beyond wishing and praying for.

Meanwhile the room had grown quite still. There was the sound of gentle movement in the beds, and he thought he heard the two kissing. He wanted to go away and did not dare, the silence was so perfect. It came heavily home to him that things had not been so beautiful between his parents—no such fond closeness between them, although each was proud of the other and although, in the face of the world, they stood firmly side by side, and jealously guarded each other's honour and public respect. He could not get clear in his mind as to what his parents lacked. Then the two in the room began to say the Lord's Prayer together, and Andreas stole away.

Now more than ever he felt drawn to Romana's room, irresistibly, yet differently from before, everything stood out clear in black and white. He said to himself: one day this will be my house, my wife, then I shall lie beside her talking about our children. He was sure now that she was waiting for him, just as he was going to her, for many innocent, glowing embraces, and a secret betrothal.

With quick, sure steps he approached the door: it was ajar, and yielded noiselessly to his pressure. He felt that she was sitting awake in the dark, aglow with expectation. He was already in the middle of the room when he noticed that she did not move. Her breath came and went so soundlessly that he had to hold his own as he strained to listen, and could not tell whether she was awake or asleep. His shadow lay as if rooted to the floor; in his impatience he all but whispered her name, to wake her with kisses if no answer came—then he felt as if a cold knife had pierced him. In another bed, over which a cupboard cast black shadow, another sleeper stirred, sighed, turned over. The head came near the moonlight—white-streaked hair. It was the old maidservant, the nurse. Then he had to go; between each step and the next, time stretched endlessly. Frustrated, as in a dream, he stole along the long moonlit corridor to his room.

He felt more at ease, more at home, than ever before in his life. He looked out over the back courtyard; the full moon was hanging over the stable, it was a glassy clear night. The dog was standing in the full moonlight, holding its head strangely, away to one side, and in this posture was turning round and round on itself. The creature seemed to be suffering horribly—perhaps it was old and very near death. Andreas was seized with dull pain; a sadness beyond all measure possessed him to see the animal suffering when he was so happy, as though the sight were a premonition of the approaching death of his father.

He left the window. He could think of his Romana again, but now more truly and solemnly, since he had just thought of his parents in the same way. He was soon undressed and in bed, and in his imagination was writing to his parents. Thoughts poured in upon him, every argument that occurred to him was unanswerable, they had never had such a letter from him. They must feel that he was no longer a boy now, but a man. If he had been a daughter instead of a son—he began somewhat in this way—they would long ago have known the joy, while still hale, of embracing their grandchildren and seeing their children's children growing up. Because of him they had had to wait too long for that joy; it was one of the purest joys of life, and in a way itself a renewal of life. His parents had never had much joy from him—the thought was as vivid as if they were dead, and he must lay himself upon them to warm them with his body. Now they had sent him on a costly journey to a foreign land. Why? To see foreign peoples, to observe foreign customs, to polish his manners. But all these things were means, means to one end. How much better it would be if this supreme end, which was nothing more nor less than his life's happiness, could be reached by one sudden step! Now, by God's sudden guidance, he had found the girl, the life-mate to make that happiness secure. From then on he had but one aim—by her side to content his parents by his own content.

The letter he wrote in his imagination far surpassed this poor abstract; the most moving words came unsought, a chain of beautiful phrases formed of itself. He spoke of the fine estate of the Finazzer family, and of their ancient and noble descent, without boasting, but in a way which really pleased him. If he had a pen and ink-well at hand he would have jumped out of bed and had the letter written at a sitting. But then fatigue began to dissolve the beautiful chain, other visions thrust themselves between, and all brought horror and dread.

It might have been a little past midnight. He sank into one confused and ugly dream after another. All the humiliations he had ever suffered in his life, everything that had ever caused him pain and fear, came over him again. He had to relive all the troubled and false situations of his life as a child and boy. And Romana fled before him, strangely dressed, half peasant, half lady, barefoot under her black pleated brocade skirt, and it was in Vienna, in the crowded Spiegelgasse, quite close to his parents' home. He had to follow her, in dread, and yet, in dread, conceal his hurried pursuit. She forced her way through the crowd, turned her face to him, and it was expressionless and distorted. As she sped on, her clothes were torn in disorder from her body. Suddenly she vanished in an entry, and he after her, as far as he could with his left foot, which dragged intolerably and kept catching between the paving stones. Now at last he was in the entry, and here no

horrible encounter was spared him. A look that he
had feared more than any other as a boy, the look of
his first catechist, shot through him, and the dreaded
little podgy hand seized him. The loathsome face of
a boy, who had told him on the backstairs in the
twilight what he did not want to hear, was pressed
close to his cheek, and as he struggled to push it
away he saw lying in front of the door through
which he had to follow Romana a creature which
moved after him: it was the cat whose back he had
once broken with a cart shaft, and which had taken
so long to die. And so it was not dead, after all these
years! Creeping like a snake with its broken back it
came towards him, and panic seized him as it looked
at him. There was no help for it. He had to step
over it. With unspeakable torment he raised his left
foot over the creature, whose back writhed up and
down unceasingly—when the look of the cat's upturned face struck him from below, the roundness of
the cat's face from a head at once cat and dog, filled
with a horrible mixture of sensual gratification and
death agony—he opened his mouth to scream—a
scream issued from the house: he had to writhe his
way through the wardrobe, which was full of his
parents' clothes. The screams from within grew more
horrible, as though a living creature were being
butchered by a murderer. It was Romana, and he

could not help her. There were too many worn-out clothes, the clothes of many years, which had not been given away. Dripping with sweat, he writhed his way through....

He was lying in bed, his heart pounding. It was already dawn, but not yet day. The house was astir, doors were banging, from the courtyard came a noise of hurrying steps and loud voices. Then the screaming began again which had torn his dreaming soul from the depths of his dream to the livid light. It was the piercing weeping and wailing of a woman's voice—a shrill complaint ceaselessly rising and falling. Andreas leapt out of bed and dressed, but he felt like a condemned man awakened by the voice of the executioner: he was still too much in his dream—it was as if he had committed some dreadful deed, and now everything would come to light.

He ran downstairs in the direction of the voice ringing so dreadfully through the house. Thinking it might be Romana, his blood froze. Then he knew that no such sounds could issue from her though she was being roasted alive in martyrdom.

Downstairs, on the ground floor, a little passage leading sideways was full of farm hands and maids staring in at the open door of a room. Andreas joined them and they made way for him. On the threshold of the room he stopped. Smoke and a stench of burning rose towards him. A half-naked woman was tied to the bed-post, and from her mouth burst the ceaseless, piercing complaints or imprecations, such as the damned in hell might utter, which had penetrated to the depths of Andreas's dream. The farmer was busying himself about the raving creature; his wife, half dressed, beside him; the steward was cutting with his pocket-knife the knotted rope which bound her ankles to the bed. The cords from her hands and a gag lay on the floor. The head maid was pouring water from a jug on to the smouldering mattress and the charred posts at the head of the bed, and stamping out the glowing sparks in the straw and twigs piled up beside the bed.

Then Andreas recognized in the screaming woman bound there the young maid who had been carrying on with his servant the day before, and a frightful foreboding made his blood run cold. The half-demented woman seemed to be calming down, reassured by the farmer and his wife. Twitching, she lay across the knees of the housekeeper, who wrapped her up in a horse-rug. She began to answer the farmer's questions; her swollen face took on a human expression, but every answer turned to a soul-rending shriek, which forced its way from her distended mouth and rang though the house. Had the man stunned her with a blow, or in some other way, and then gagged her? asked the farmer. What kind of poison had been mixed for the dog? Had a long or short time passed since she had contrived to tear the gag out of her mouth? But the woman could utter nothing except that she had screamed with horror for a just God to hear her: he had tied her up like that, had made up the fire under her very eyes, and bolted her in from the outside, had grinned in at her through the window and taunted her in her deadly fear. And all mixed with imploring prayers to forgive her her grievous sin. No name was spoken, but Andreas knew only too well whom they were speaking about. As though he had seen what he had come to see, he passed like a sleepwalker through the crowd of farm hands and maids, who silently made way for him; behind them all, cowering in a doorway, stood Romana, half dressed, barefoot and trembling—almost as I saw her in my dream, something in him said. When she became aware of him her face took on an expression of boundless horror.

He went into the stable; a young groom followed him, perhaps suspicious. The stall where Andreas's chestnut had stood the day before was empty; the bay stood in its misery. The tall young groom, who had an honest face, looked at Andreas, who forced himself to ask: "Did he take anything else with him?"

"It doesn't seem so for the moment," said the

groom. "A few of us are after him, but his horse is certainly the faster, and he's had as much as two hours' start."

Andreas said nothing. His horse was gone, and with it more than half his journey money which was sewn into the saddle. But that seemed nothing compared with the shame of standing thus before the farmer's people, into whose house he had brought this horror. The saying: "Like master, like man," came into his mind, and then, like a lightning flash, the saying reversed, so that he stood as if drenched with blood before the honest face of the lad.

"The horse there was stolen from us too," said the groom, pointing to the bay. "The master knew it at once, but he didn't want to say anything about it at first."

Andreas made no answer. He went upstairs, and without counting what money he had left, he took out as much as he thought would repay Finazzer for his stolen property. As he had no idea what a horse like the bay might fetch among the country folk, he put into his pocket as much as he had paid for it in Villach to make sure. Then he stood in unconscious thought for a long time by the table in his room, and at last went downstairs to settle the affair.

He had to wait before he could speak to the farmer, for the three men who had ridden in pursuit had just come back, and were reporting what they had seen and what they had found out from the shepherds and wayfarers they had met; but there was little likelihood of laying hands on the scoundrel. The farmer was kind and composed, Andreas all the more embarrassed.

"Then do you want to keep the horse and buy it from me a second time? For I'm sure you've paid honestly for it."

Andreas said no.

"If not, how can I take your money? You have brought back my stolen property; besides, through you I know there is a bad girl in the stable, so that I can get her out of the house and into the hands of the law before she does more mischief. You are an inexperienced young gentleman, and our Lord had His hand visibly over you. The maid has confessed that when she was with the ruffian she saw a brand on his shoulder, and she thinks that if he had not caught her looking at it, for he turned as white as chalk when he did, he would not have used her so savagely. Thank your Maker that He has preserved you from spending a night in the woods with a run-away murderer. If you mean to go on to Italy, there is a carrier passing here this evening. He will take you to Villach, and from there you will find an opportunity of travelling down to Venice any day."

THE CARRIER did not arrive until the following evening, and so Andreas spent two more days at the Finazzer farm. It was terrible to him to be on the farmer's hands after such an affair: he felt like a prisoner. He crept about the house, the people went about their work, nobody heeded him. Through a window he saw the farmer in the distance mount and ride away: he had no further sight of the wife. He went out of the house and up the fields behind the farm. The clouds were hanging low over the valley, the whole world was dreary and heavy, and as desolate as the end of time. He did not know where to go, sat down on a stack of wood. He tried to imagine other weather, but it seemed to him as if this valley could only look as it did now. "And yet I was so happy here yesterday," he said. He tried to recall Romana's face, but could not, and at once gave up the attempt. "Such a thing could only happen to you," he heard his father's voice saying, as sharp and clear as if it were outside him. He stood up, took a few heavy steps, the voice said it again. "Why do I believe it myself?" he brooded, and with dragging feet he went slowly up the path; yet it was dreadful to him because he had been that way yesterday. Not that he had any thought of Romana: it was only the intolerably distinct feeling of yesterday, of the afternoon hour, which had been followed by the evening, the night, and this morning hour. "Why do I know myself that it had to happen to me?" he brooded on, looking up now and then at the wooded slopes beyond, with the mist lying about them, as a prisoner looks up at the walls of his cell.

Thus dully brooding he counted up his expenses for the four days' journey from Vienna to Villach, which now seemed exorbitant, then the money for the second horse and the stolen sum. Then he worked out what was left from Austrian into Venetian money: in sequins it seemed scanty enough, but in dou-bloons so beggarly that he stopped and wondered whether to turn back or travel farther. In his present state of mind he would have turned back, but his parents would never have forgiven him, as so much money had been squandered for absolutely nothing. He seemed to feel as if his parents were not really concerned with him, and his happiness, but only with outward show and what people would say. The faces of friends and relations rose before him; among them some were malicious and bloated, some indif-ferent, some even kindly, but there was not one the sight of whom warmed his heart.

He thought of his grandfather Ferschengelder, who had been called Andreas, like him, and of how he had once tramped off from his father's farm down the Danube towards Vienna with nothing but a silver groat tied up in his handkerchief, and of how he had risen to be an Imperial Lackey-in-Ordinary, with a title. He had been a handsome man, and Andreas had his stature, though none of his bearing. He remembered the taunt that he had nothing of his grandfather, who was the pride of the family, but that it was his Uncle Leopold that he took after. He too as a child had been cruel to animals, and had grown up to be a violent, unhappy wretch, who wasted his substance, could not maintain the honour of the family, and had brought nothing but grief and trouble on those who had had to do with him.

His Uncle Leopold's thickset figure rose before him, his red face and bulging eyes. He saw him lying on his deathbed, the arms of the Ferschengelders on a wooden scutcheon at his feet. Through one door, flung open by a servant, came the childless, legitimate wife, a Della Spina by birth, with a handkerchief in her beautiful, high-born hand; through the other half-open door slipped in the other, illegitimate wife, the round-faced peasant woman with the pretty double chin, her six children holding hands behind her, and gazing timidly past their mother at their dead, noble father. And as is generally the way with those in sorrow and darkness, in memory Andreas envied the dead man.

Turning back to the farm he began again to

reckon by how much the portion of the Ferschen-gelders had dwindled; he counted up how much of their present income had been sacrificed to his journey, and fell a prey to morbid imaginings. At the dinner-table he found his place set, but today, at the head of the table, the old, white-haired maid sat and served. Not only was the farmer absent, but his wife and Romana too. Andreas felt that he had always known it would be so; he felt that he would not see Romana again. He ate in silence, the servants talked to each other, but none let fall a word about the event of the night. It transpired that the farmer had ridden to Villach to speak to the magistrate. The steward, as he stood up, said to Andreas across the table that the farmer had left a message for him: the carrier might possibly not pass that way until the next day. In that case, Andreas would be so good as to stay on, and to excuse his absence.

It was a cheerless, still afternoon. Andreas would have given anything for a breath of wind. The mist had rolled together into clouds, big and small: they hung there motionless, as if from everlasting to everlasting. Andreas once more mounted the path towards the village. The thought of going downhill was repugnant to him: he could not have borne the return uphill with the Finazzer farm ahead. He knew no road on the other side of the valley. If he only had a companion—a farm dog, or some animal. I have thrown that away for ever, he said to himself.

The only thought that came to him was a torment. He saw himself as a twelve-year-old boy, saw the little stray dog following his every step. The humility with which it took him, the first being it met, as its master, the joy, the bliss with which it moved if he so much as looked at it, were past understanding. If it thought its master was angry it would roll on its back, draw up its little legs anxiously, yield itself utterly, with an indescribable expression in its upturned eyes. One day Andreas saw it in front of a big dog in the posture he thought it took only for him, to soothe his anger and win his good graces. His blood rose, he called the dog to him. Ten paces off it became aware of his angry look. And it came creeping on, its tremulous eyes fixed on Andreas's face. He taunted it for a low, cowardly beast, and under his taunts it crept closer and closer. It seemed to him that he raised his foot and struck the creature's spine with his heel. The dog gave a yelp of pain and collapsed, still wagging its tail. He turned on his heel and went away. The dog crept after him; its loins were broken, yet it crawled after its master like a snake, its back giving at every step. At last he stopped; the little dog fixed its eyes on him, wagged its tail, and died. He was not sure whether he had done the thing or not—but it issued from him. Thus the infinite touched him. The memory was torture, yet he felt a wave of home-sickness for the twelve-year-old Andreas who had done it. Everything seemed good that was not here, everything worth living that was not the present. Below him he saw a Capuchin tramping along the road. Before a crucifix he knelt. How serene his untrammelled soul must be! With his thoughts Andreas took refuge in the figure, till it vanished at a bend in the road. Then he was alone again.

He could not bear the valley; he climbed up to the wood. He felt better among the tree-trunks. Damp twigs struck his face, he bounded forward, rotting branches crackled under him on the ground. He measured his bounds so that with each he was hidden behind massive tree-trunks: there were old maples and beeches still standing among the pines, and he hid behind each of them, then bounded on, until he had escaped from himself, as from a prison. He leapt on—he knew nothing of himself save the moment. Now he thought he was Uncle Leopold pursuing a peasant girl like a faun in the forest, now that he was a criminal and murderer like Gotthilff, with the sheriff's men after him. But he contrived to elude them—fell on his knees before the Empress....

All at once he felt that a human being was really watching from close by. So even this was poisoned! He crouched behind a hazel-bush, as still as an animal. The man in the little clearing, fifty paces in front of him, was peering into the wood. When he had heard nothing for a while he went on with his work. He was digging. Andreas leapt towards him from tree to tree. When a twig cracked the man outside looked up from his work, but at last Andreas came quite close to him. It was one of the farm hands from Castell Finazzer. He buried the house dog, then threw the earth back into the grave, flattened it down with his spade, and went away.

Andreas threw himself on to the grave and lay for a long time in heavy thought. "Here!" he said to himself. "Here! All this wandering about is futile, we cannot escape from ourselves. We are dragged hither and thither, they sent me all this long way—at last it comes to an end somewhere—here!" There was something between him and the dog, he did not know what, just as there was something between him and Gotthilff, who had brought about the dog's death. Threads ran to and fro, and out of them a world was woven, behind the real one, and not so empty and desolate. Then he was amazed at himself: "Why am I here?" And he felt as if another man were lying there, and that he must enter into him, but had forgotten the word.

Evening had fallen without a gleam of red in the sky, without any of the signs with which the beauty of the changing day is made manifest. From the heavy clouds a dismal gloom descended, and from the misty air a quiet rain began to fall on Andreas as he lay on the grave. He felt cold, rose, and went down.

In his dream that night the sun was shining. He went deeper and deeper into the forest and found Romana. The deeper he went into the forest the brighter it shone: in the middle, where everything was darkest and most radiant, he found her sitting on a little island meadow, round which shining water flowed. She had fallen asleep hay-making, her sickle and rake beside her. As he stepped over the water she looked up at him, but as she would look at a stranger. He called to her: "Romana, can you see me?" Her eyes moved so vacantly.

"Why, yes, of course," she said. "Do you know, I don't know where the dog is buried."

He felt strange, could not help laughing at what she said. She shrank from him in fear, stumbled into the heap of hay and sank half down on to the ground like a wounded doe. He was close to her and felt that she took him for the wicked Gotthilff, and yet not for Gotthilff either, and he himself was not quite sure who he was. She besought him not to tie her naked to the bed in front of all the people, and not to run away on a stolen horse. He took hold of her, called her tenderly by her name—she was distraught with fear. He let her go: she struggled after him on her knees.

"Come back! I will go with you, if it were to the gallows. Father wants to lock me in, mother has her arms around me, my dead brothers and sisters are trying to cling to me too, but I'll get away, I'll leave them all to come to you." He tried to reach her, but she had vanished.

In despair he rushed into the wood—and she came to meet him between two beautiful maples, as friendly and kind as if nothing had happened. Her eyes shone with a strange lustre, her feet were luminous on the moss, and the hem of her dress was wet.

"What kind of woman are you?" he cried.

"This kind," she said, holding up her mouth to him. "No, this kind!" she cried, as he stretched out his arms to embrace her, striking at him with her rake. She struck him on the forehead, there was a sharp, clear sound as if a pane of glass had broken. He awoke with a start.

He knew that he had been dreaming, but the truth in his dream filled him with joy to the last fibre. Romana's whole being had been revealed to him with a vividness that was more than life. All his heaviness was dispelled. Within him or without he could not lose her. He had the knowledge—even more, the faith, that she lived for him. He returned to the world like one blessed. He felt that she might be standing below, had thrown a stone at the window pane and awakened him. He ran to the window; a pane was cracked, a dead bird lay on the sill. He went slowly back, the bird in his hand, and laid it on his pillow. The little body poured delight through his veins, he felt as if he could easily have restored the bird to life if he had only taken it to his heart. He sat on the bed, a thousand thoughts streamed round him, he was happy. His body was a temple in which Romana's being dwelt, and time in its flow swept round him, and lapped on the steps of the temple.

In the house everything was at first still in the greying morning, and rain was falling. When he arose from his dreaming ecstasy, day had come and it was light. The whole house was at work. He went downstairs, asked for a piece of bread and drank from the fountain. He wandered about the house, nobody heeded him. Wherever he was, whatever he did, he was at ease: his soul had a centre. He took his food with the people, the farmer had not returned, nobody mentioned the wife or Romana. In the afternoon the carrier arrived. He was ready to take Andreas with him, but to judge from the way his business was going, he would have to leave before evening: they would spend the night in the next village down the valley.

A fresh wind was blowing into the valley, beautiful, big clouds were driving across it, and beyond, over the country, all was shining clear. A farm-hand carried the portmanteau and valise down to the cart, Andreas followed him. At the bottom of the stairs he turned back, and a voice told him that Romana was standing waiting up in his empty room. When he entered the room and found it empty, he could hardly believe it; he searched every corner, as though she might be hidden in the whitewashed wall. With bent head he went downstairs again. There he stood for a while irresolute, listening. Outside the grooms were talking as they helped to put the horses in. Andreas felt his breast contract. Without his will his feet carried him to the stable. The bay was standing there looking dejected, with its ears laid back; a few of the farm horses turned in their stalls as Andreas came in. Andreas stood—he did not know how long—in the dim place, listening to a twittering—then through the little barred window a shaft of gold shot slanting to the stable door, and hung there, a swallow glided through, flashing, and behind it Romana's mouth, open, moist and

twitching with suppressed weeping. He could hardly
grasp that she was standing bodily before him, but
he did grasp it, and the fulness of his heart paralysed
his limbs. She was barefoot, her plaits were hanging
down as if she had that moment jumped out of bed
and run to him. He could and would not ask, but his
arms half rose towards her. She did not come to
him, nor did she shrink from him. She was as close
to him as if she were part of him, and yet it was as if
she did not see him. In any case, she did not look at
him, and he made no move to approach her. Her
mouth struggled with the words, her eyes with the
tears that would not come. She pulled ceaselessly at
her thin silver chain, as if she were trying to strangle
herself, so as to withdraw from him utterly. It was as
though pain were having its way with her, so that
she did not even feel that Andreas was near. At last
the chain broke—one piece slid into the bosom of
her open gown, the other stayed in her hand. She
pressed it from above on to the back of Andreas's
hand; her mouth twitched as if a scream must come
and could not. She leaned against him; her mouth,
moist and twitching, kissed his—then she was gone.

The piece of silver chain had slipped from Andreas's
hand. He picked it up out of the straw—he did not
know whether to follow her—everything was happening outside him, and at the same time in the very

depths of his heart, where, till now, nothing that was not himself had ever pierced him—then he heard them looking for him outside. A crisis had come. Now, the thought flashed through him: turn everything upside-down, tell them I'm going to stay, have the luggage taken down, tell the farm hands I've changed my mind. But how could he? How could he appear before Finazzer, even before his wife? What should he say, what reasons should he give? What kind of a man would he have had to be to take this upon himself and then stand his ground in a situation so suddenly reversed?

HE WAS already sitting in the cart; the horses had started, he did not know how. Time must pass; I cannot stay here, but I can come back, he thought, the same and yet different. He felt between his fingers the chain, that assured him that it was all reality and not a dream.

The cart rolled downhill; in front of him was the sun and the wide, sunlit country, behind him the narrow valley with the lonely homestead already lying in the shadow. His eyes were fixed ahead, but with a vacant, close look; the eyes of his heart were looking backwards with all their might. He was roused by the voice of the carrier, who was pointing with his whip up into the pure evening air where an

eagle was wheeling. Now for the first time Andreas
was aware of what lay before him. The road had
wound out of the mountain valley and taken a sudden turn to the left. There a huge valley had opened;
a river, no longer a brook, wound far below, but
beyond it was the mightiest peak of the range, behind
which, still high in the sky, the sun was sinking.
Monstrous shadows fell down into the valley; whole
forests, blackish blue, bristled on the riven foot of the
mountain; waterfalls plunged darkly down in the
ravines; above everything was free, bare, rising boldly
upwards—sheer slopes, rock walls, crowned by the
snowy peak, ineffably pure and radiant.

Never had Andreas known such a feeling in nature.
He felt as if it had all, at a single stroke, risen from
his own being—that power, that uprising and its
crowning purity. The majestic bird was still wheeling
above, alone in the light; with widespread wings it
swept slow circles; from where it hovered it could see
everything—the Finazzer valley and the farm, the
village; the graves of Romana's sisters and brothers
were as near to its keen sight as these mountain
gorges, in whose bluish shadows it was searching for
a young roe or a stray goat. Andreas encompassed
the bird—he rose towards it with a feeling of ecstasy.
This time he felt no impulse to lose himself, he only
felt the bird's supreme power and gift flowing into

his own soul. Every shadow, every clog, fell away from him. It was borne in upon him that, seen from high enough, the parted are united, and that loneliness is an illusion. He possessed Romana everywhere—he could take her into him wherever he would. That mountain, rising before him and towering to the skies, was a brother and more than a brother. As it took the tender fawn to its breast in its mighty spaces, covering it with cool shade, and hiding it from its pursuer with blue darkness, so Romana lived in him. She was a living being, a centre, with a paradise about her no more unreal than the one towering up beyond the valley. He looked into himself, and saw Romana kneel down to pray: she bent her knees as the fawn, when it lies down to rest, folds its tender legs, and the movement was ineffably dear to him. Circles dissolved in circles. He prayed with her, and when he looked, he knew that the mountain was simply his prayer. An unutterable certainty came home to him. It was the happiest moment of his life.

WHEN HE came downstairs to rejoin the people of the house he found the girl Zustina busily arguing with a small, middle-aged man, whose almost crescent-shaped nose gave him a curiously dashing, appearance, and who had in his hand something in a cotton handkerchief which filled the room with the smell of fish.

"No, really, it cannot go on, the way you let people palm things off on you," he heard her say. "If it were another day I would manage mother. But really, today you must take it back, and don't forget the decorator. Argue it out with him, point by point, just as I told you. Decorators are a cunning lot, and have no conscience, but a man who can talk like you ought to be a match for anybody. The draw will be exactly a week after Lady Day, so that everything must be delivered the day before. If a single thing is missing a silver ducat will be struck off his pay. I want it exactly like a Corpus Christi altar, with drapery and wreaths in front, and the urn with the lottery tickets in the middle between arrangements of fresh flowers. He's to charge no extras for putting it up. He's to bring it here, and Zorzi will have to help in the arranging and decorating. Now go and tell him all that so that we may be proud of you, and leave your book here. I will cast it up."

The old man was going away as Andreas entered. "Oh, there you are," said Zustina. "Your luggage has just arrived, Zorzi will fetch men to carry it up. Then he will show you a good coffee-house, and take you to my sister's if you like. She will be glad to see you. He's useful for errands of that kind," she added. "For that matter, there is absolutely no need for you to make a bosom friend of him at once. But after all, that's your business. It takes all kinds to make a world, and we all have to get through it as best we can. What I say is, you must take the world as you find it."

She ran to the stove, looked into the oven, basted the meat; a number of garments, which seemed to belong to her mother and brothers, vanished into a big cupboard. She chased the cat off the table, and attended to a bird hanging in a cage in the window. "There was something else I wanted to say to you," she went on, coming to a stand-still in front of Andreas. "I don't know whether you have much money on you, or a letter to a banker. If it's money, then give it to a business friend or anyone you happen to know in the town to keep for you. Not that there are dishonest people in the house, but I won't take the responsibility. I've got enough to do to keep the house tidy and teach my two brothers and look after my father, for my mother generally works away from home. Besides, you can imagine how much I have to work and plan to get ready for the lottery. How easily offended... I'm sorry we can't possibly offer you a ticket, even though you are in the house, but you are a foreigner, and our patrons are very particular in these things. The second prize is very nice too—it's a gold and enamel snuff-box. I'll show it to you as soon as it comes home from the jewellers."

Meanwhile she added up the little account book, using for the purpose a tiny pencil which she had hidden in one of the curls of her *toupet*, for her hair was dressed as it might be for a ball, in a high *toupet*. She wore cloth slippers, a taffeta skirt, with silver lace, but over it a checked dressing-jacket which was much too big for her and left completely bare her charmingly slender, yet by no means childish, throat. Amid the half-exclamations with which she inter-spersed her talk, her eyes darted from Andreas to the stove and the cat. Suddenly something flashed through her mind; she flew to the window, leant far out, and called shrilly down: "Count Gasparo, Count Gasparo —listen! I've got something to say to you."

"Here I am," said the man with the hooked nose and the fish, unexpectedly coming through the door into the room. "Why scream at me through the win-dow? Here I am"—and he turned to Andreas. "I have only just heard below that you are the young foreign nobleman whom I have the honour to wel-come as my guest. I wish both for your and our own sakes that you may be happy under our humble roof. You occupy the rooms of my daughter Nina. You do not yet know her, and so you cannot yet appreciate the proof of respect and confidence we have given you in placing that apartment at your disposal. The room of such a being is like the robe of a saint—it harbours powers. Whatever you may experience in this town—and you have come here to gather knowledge and experience—within those walls peace will re-enter your mind, and steadiness your soul. The very air of those rooms breathes—how shall I put it?—virtue invincible. Rather die than sacrifice that virtue was the iron resolve of my child. I, sir"—he touched Andreas with his hand, which was white and extremely shapely, but too small for a man and hence displeasing—"was in a position neither to strengthen my child in such a resolve nor to reward her for it. Mine is a wrecked existence. Storms have hurled me from the summit of my family." He withdrew, letting his hand sink with an inimitable gesture. With a bow he left the room.

Zustina's face was radiant with admiration at the Count's speech. And indeed the manner in which he had pronounced these few sentences was a masterpiece of decorum and condescension. Dignity was mingled with humanity; gravity and experience were tempered with confidence. The elder spoke to the younger, the host to his guest, the old man tried by life spoke as a father to the untried youth, and the Venetian nobleman to a nobleman—it was all there. "What do you think of my father's way of speaking?"

she asked. In her sincere and childish pleasure she seemed to have forgotten that she had called him back for anything at all. "That's the way," she cried, "he finds the tone to suit every occasion. He has had a great deal of trouble, and many enemies, but no one can deny his great talents." While before she had been quicksilvery and eager, but tart, she was now kindled from within; her eyes flashed and her mouth moved with an indescribable, childlike zest. There was something of the squirrel about her, yet she was a resolute, honest little woman.

"So now you know my father too, and before an hour has passed you will know my sister, and some of her friends too, for certain. The most distinguished of them all is the Duke of Camposagrado, the Spanish ambassador. He is such a great gentleman that when the King of Spain speaks to him he puts his hat on. Don't be startled when you see him: he looks like a wild beast, but he's a very great gentleman. Then there's one of her friends I would like myself—but why speak about me? He's an Austrian officer, a Slavonian; that means he has an Austrian captain's commission and perquisites, the cattle import duties on Hungarian and Styrian oxen coming in by Trieste—a fine business. He's a handsome man too, and madly in love with Nina. Just think— he never gets up from the table without drinking her health and then, every time, throwing his glass through the window pane into the canal or against the wall; but when it's a special day he simply breaks all the glass on the table, just in honour of Nina. Of course, he pays for the glasses afterwards. Isn't it savage? But in his country it's the highest courtesy. He's a great gambler—however, you will get to know him yourself. If he were my husband I would soon break him of it.

"But one thing," she went on, looking at him with a charming expression of gravity and importance, "if you get mixed up in disputes, misunderstandings, quarrels, and so on, get your own way. Don't let anybody, man or woman, get round you with tears. That's a silly weakness and I can't bear it. But I'm not speaking about Nina's tears. Nina's tears are as real as gold. When she cries she's like a little child. Nobody has the heart to refuse her what she wants, for she's ten times kinder than I am, although she is twenty-one, and I'm not sixteen yet. But how can it interest you," she added, with an arch look, as she busied herself about the bird in the cage, "to hear me talking about myself? You didn't come to Venice for that. Go downstairs. Zorzi will be waiting for you down there."

Andreas was already on the stairs when she came after him. "One thing more—it just occurred to me.

You look good-natured, and a good man must be warned at the first step. Don't let anybody inveigle you into accepting his bills, even though he should offer you at the same time others to cover them which are due before his. Never. Do you understand me?" For an instant her hand rested lightly on Andreas's arm. It was exactly the same gesture as her father had made before, yet how much truth there is in the saying that if two do the same thing the result is world's apart. The little hand was so charming and the motherly, womanly gesture enchanting. She was already back in the house, and as Andreas went downstairs he heard her calling to Zorzi on the other side through the window.

"Isn't she a lovely little thing?" said Zorzi, who was standing below, as if he had guessed what was busying Andreas's thoughts.

"But what is all this about the lottery?" asked Andreas, after a few steps. "Who distributes the prizes and what has the family got to do with it? It looks as if they were organizing it themselves."

The artist did not reply at once. "And so they are," he said, slackening his pace at a street corner to let Andreas catch up with him. "Why shouldn't I tell you? The lottery is being arranged in a circle of rich and distinguished gentlemen, and the first prize is the girl herself."

"How do you mean—the girl herself?"

"Well, her virginity, if you want another word for it. She's a good girl, and has taken it into her head to rescue her family from their poverty. You ought to hear how nicely she speaks about it, and how much trouble she has taken with the subscription list. For whatever she does must be done properly. A great gentleman, a friend of the family, has taken over the patronage." Here he lowered his voice. "He is the patrician, Signor Sacramozo, who was lately Governor of Corfu. A ticket costs no less than twenty-four sequins, and not a name has been put on the subscription list that has not been approved by Signor Sacramozo."

Andreas had suddenly blushed with such violence that a haze blurred his eyesight, and he nearly slipped on a squashed pomegranate lying in his way. The other looked at him sidelong as he walked. "An affair of this kind," he went on, "can be arranged in a circle of men of breeding who have the decency not to let it get abroad, otherwise the authorities would intervene. So the gentlemen of the town would be rather unwilling to let a foreigner into an arrangement of the kind. But if you really care about it, I'll do what I can for you, and perhaps I could get a ticket for you indirectly. I mean in this way, that one of the ticket-holders, for a consideration, which won't be small, might hand over his chance to you without your name being mentioned." Andreas did not know what to answer, and quickly changed the subject by saying how astonished he was that the elder daughter should know no better way of coming to her family's help, and leave it to the little sister to sacrifice herself in so unusual a fashion.

"Well, it isn't really so unusual, what she's doing," returned the other, "and there's nothing much to be hoped for from Nina. The little one knows that better than anybody. Nina can't manage money, and what you give her today melts between her fingers tomorrow. She's a beauty, but she's no match for Zustina in brains. I'll give you an instance: once I wanted to present to her a rich and noble gentleman from Vienna, Count Grassalkowicz—you'll know the name. And you'll know what it means to make the acquaintance of a man who, as you know, has two palaces in Vienna and one in Prague, and whose estates in Croatia are as big as all the possessions of the Republic. 'What's the man's name?' says she, drawing up her nose, and when she does that there's no more to be got out of her than out of a shying horse. 'The name,' she says, 'sounds like a common oath, and the man will be like it. Take him where you like. I won't have anything to do with him.' That's Nina all over."

Andreas thought that it was no such extraordinary distinction as he had imagined to be introduced to Signorina Nina, and by this friend, but he kept his thoughts to himself.

They had reached an open square with wooden tables and wicker chairs in front of a little coffee-stall. At one of them a man dressed all in black was writing letters. At another a coarse middle-aged man with a blue chin, wearing an odd kind of long frogged coat, sat at his ease, listening unmoved to the pleadings of a young man who did not venture to draw up his chair to the table, and hardly even dared to sit down, so that Andreas could not look at him without a feeling of pity and distress.

"Look at those two," said Zorzi, taking possession of the chocolate Andreas had ordered for him. "That's a rich Greek and his nephew. The old man is a millionaire, and the poor lad is his only relation. But he isn't pleased with him because the young man married against his will, and he won't let him into his house. The young man can hardly keep his head above water. He's in the hands of moneylenders, Jews and Christians, and is always running after his uncle. Take a quiet look at them: the old man will hardly deign to see him, let alone give him an answer. He goes on smoking and lets him talk—look how the miserable beggar is wriggling for fear of getting so much as the smell of his smoke. And after a while, you'll see, he'll pay for his coffee and go away, and in the end the young man will fall on his knees before him, and the old man will take no more notice of him than if he were a dog. He'll hang on his coat, and the old man will shake him off and go on his way as if he were alone. You can see the same show several times a day, in the morning in front of the Exchange here, and in the evening on the Riva. Isn't it amusing to see what beasts people can be to each other, and how obstinate they can be in their spite?"

Andreas was hardly listening, so preoccupied was he by the appearance of the man writing. He had an inordinately long, narrow body, which, as he wrote, stooped over the table, under which his long legs could only find room as it were by apology, inordinately long arms which could, at a pinch, find room, and inordinately long fingers which held the bad, squeaking pen. His posture was uncomfortable and even ridiculous, but nothing could have more finely revealed the essence of the man than this discomfort, and the way he bore it, overcame it, was unaware of it. He wrote hurriedly, the breeze tugged at the page, he ought to have lost his temper, and yet there was self-command in all his limbs, a—so strange as the word may seem—courtesy towards all the lifeless objects which rendered him such sorry service, a superiority to the discomfort of the situation which was incomparable. A strong gust blew one of the sheets over to Andreas. Andreas started up, and hastened to return it to the stranger, who, turning quietly round, took the proffered sheet with a slight bow. Andreas met his dark eyes; he thought them beautiful, although they were set in a face that nobody could call handsome. The head was far too small for the figure, and the sallow, rather sickly face so strangely awry that the absurd image of the shrunken face of a dead toad flashed through Andreas's mind.

He would have liked to know a great deal about the man, but he did not want to learn it from Zorzi, who bent towards him and whispered: "I'll tell you who that is as soon as he's gone. I don't want to mention his name now. He's the brother—well, the brother of the great gentleman whom I told you was the protector of the family you're living with. You know whom I mean—the one under whose aegis the lottery is being arranged. He is a Knight of Malta," he went on, but at once paused as the writer raised his head, "but as you see, he doesn't wear on his cloak the cross which it is not only his right, but his duty to wear. He has travelled a great deal, they say; he has been far into the interior of India, and even at the Great Wall of China, and some say he is in the service of the Jesuits, but others say he is no more than a freemason."

The rich Greek and his beggarly nephew stood up—the gross callousness of the one, the bestial servility of the other, were revolting. In both, human nature seemed to have lost its dignity. For Andreas it was past understanding that so vile a spectacle could take place in the neighbourhood of a being such as he imagined the Knight to be. When the two raised their voices, the one spitting like a cat, the other in a kind of whimper, he even felt he must rush between them and silence them with his stick. The Knight of Malta raised his eyes for a moment, but looked away over the two, as if they were not there, and, closing his letter as he rose, nodded to a lad who now ran up, took the letter with a bow, and went off with it, while the Knight walked away in the other direction.

When he had disappeared round the corner the square seemed desolate to Andreas. Zorzi bent and picked up a folded sheet of notepaper from under the table. "The wind has blown some of Knight Sacramozo's correspondence under our feet," he said. "Excuse me a moment. I'll go and take it to him."

"Let me take it," came from Andreas's mouth: his tongue seemed to say it of its own will. The fulfil-

ment of his wish meant infinitely much to him; he
snatched the paper out of the other's hand and ran
after the Knight down a narrow alley.

There was more than grace, there was a really
inimitable distinction in the way the Knight listened
to him and took the paper, and Andreas thought he
had never experienced so wonderful a harmony between the bearing of a human being and the sound
of his voice. "You are very kind, sir," came from his
lips in German, in the best pronunciation. His
genial, and at the same time spiritual face seemed to
express a profound kindliness arising from his soul.
In the space of a moment Andreas felt himself
received with benevolence, caught up into an atmosphere which elevated every fibre of his being, and
then dismissed. He stood before the stranger as if
inanimate, his body felt clumsy, his attitude uncouth.
But every limb of his body was aware of every other,
and, as flame quivers on flame, imprinted deep
within him was the image of the tall figure which,
in easy assurance, in gracious civility, bent slightly
towards him.

He went back, already striving dully within himself
to retain the expression of those eyes, the sound of
that voice, as though he had lost them for ever—
wondering, "have I ever seen him before? How else
could his image have been impressed on me in one

moment? I can learn about him from myself!" But great was his astonishment when he felt, rather than heard, swift and light steps hurrying after him, which could belong to nobody but the Knight, when he saw him catch up with him and, in the same winning voice, with the most perfect courtesy, assure him that he must have made a mistake. "The letter you were so kind as to give me, sir, is neither written by my hand nor addressed to me. It must belong to you—in any case, I must beg you to dispose of it!"

Andreas was embarrassed and confused. A few hazy thoughts crossed his mind, the fear of seeming to intrude stabbed him like a hot needle. In his predicament, he felt it at any rate easier to say something definite than to make some vague reply, for which he would never have found the words. He reddened at a sudden movement of his hands, which had already stretched out for the letter, but all the more definitely he averred that the letter most certainly did not belong to him, that it was in no way his to dispose of. The look with which the Knight at once acquiesced was rather the look of a man who will on no account insist than of one persuaded of error, and the faint shimmer of a smile played across his face, or only his eyes, as he again bowed courteously and turned away.

"It is time," said Zorzi, "if you want to meet our

lovely Nina today. She will be up, and if we are lucky will have no visitors yet. Later she drives out, or dines with her friends. Well?" he asked, as they walked, "did you make the acquaintance of the Knight, and give him back his letter? Think—the fool writes two or three such letters a day, ten pages at a time to one and the same person, though he sees her every day, and so far as I know he isn't even her lover. For she is half crazy, and is either lying ill in bed, or on her knees in some church. She has no husband, nor any other relation. The Knight is her only visitor, and as she does not go out he hasn't even the fun of passing for her cavalier. But he hides the affair from everybody, as if she were a girl or a nun."

"How do you contrive to know everybody's secrets?" asked Andreas, wondering.

"Oh, you hear all kinds of things," returned the other, with the smile Andreas had already so much disliked. "But here's the house. We'll just go up—or rather, wait here a minute. I'll run up and see how things stand and whether she will receive you."

Andreas could not be sure how long a time now passed. Perhaps the artist only stayed away as long as, in the ordinary way, he needed to go upstairs, have himself announced, and announce a visitor: perhaps he had had to wait upstairs, and a much longer time passed.

Andreas moved a few steps from the house door through which Zorzi had vanished, and went to the end of the rather narrow street. It ended in an archway, but, strangely enough, under the archway a bridge led over a canal to a little egg-shaped square with a chapel standing in it. Andreas returned, and was annoyed that he could not, after those few minutes, recognize the right house in the row of somewhat simple and uniform house fronts. The door of one, dark green, with a door-knocker in the shape of a dolphin, seemed to be the one through which Zorzi had vanished, yet the door was shut, and Andreas thought he could still see Zorzi as he stepped into a passage through an open door. Still, there was no danger of their missing each other if Andreas went back to the bridge again to have a look at the little square with the church. The street and the square were completely deserted; a step would be audible, let alone a call, or repeated calls, if Zorzi were looking for him, so he crossed the bridge. Below, on the dark water, a little boat was moored to it; not a human being was to be seen or heard; the little square had a forlorn, abandoned look.

The church was of brick, low and old: in front, on the side facing the square, it had an entrance which was little in keeping with it; broad steps bore a colonnade of white marble, and a classical pediment with an inscription. In the Latin words some of the gilded letters were capitals. Andreas tried to read a date out of them.

When he again lowered his eyes a woman was standing some distance away, to the side of the church, looking at him. He could not quite make out where she had come from, for she was standing rather as if she had been on her way to the church, and had stopped irresolute, or perhaps startled by Andreas's presence. He had heard no steps approaching or crossing the square, and he found himself wondering whether, with her respectable, simple dress, she wore house shoes, which had muffled her footsteps, then wondered at himself being occupied with the thought. For she was nothing more than an apparently young woman of the lower classes, with the black shawl over her head and shoulders, from whose pale, but apparently very pretty face two dark eyes were watching the stranger with a curious, and, unless distance deceived him, anxious fixity—with the same fixity, he felt, whether he now pretended to be studying the capitals of the Corinthian columns or returned the look. All the same, he had no reason to stay there, and he had already set his foot on the lowest of the stone steps, thus withdrawing from the woman's field of vision.

But when, raising the heavy curtain, he entered the church, the woman at the same time entered through a side door, and went to a *prie-dieu* standing near the altar. And now Andreas had the distinct impression that here was a woman oppressed by sickness, whether of the body or the mind, seeking relief from suffering by prayer.

He had now no other wish than to leave the church again as quietly as possible, for it seemed to him that the woman, now and then, looked anxiously round at him, as though he were an unwished-for witness of her painful solitude. Now in the church, compared with the square, which lay in the harsh sunshine, the light was dim; in the cool, stuffy air a faint smell of incense still lingered, and Andreas, who had no desire to pry, but merely to leave the place, certainly did not keep his eyes fixed on the woman perfectly clearly. However, apart from that, it was certain, he could have sworn, that she had turned, not to the altar but to his own self, with her hands clasped in entreaty, that she had even struggled to move towards him, but had been hindered, as though heavy chains lay about her body from the hips down. At the same moment he thought he clearly heard a moan: soft as it was, it could not have been an hallucination. The next moment, certainly, he could not but regard, if not the movement, then any reference to himself as imagination, for the stranger had shrunk back into the *prie-dieu* and was perfectly still.

Without a sound he crossed the short space separating him from the door, and took pains to raise the curtain so little that no ray of the harsh light should disturb the holy twilight in which he was leaving the sorrower. As he did so his eyes involuntarily sought the *prie-dieu* again, and what he now distinctly perceived astonished him so much that he stood still in the folds of the curtain, breathless. There, at exactly the same spot, sat another woman—sat no longer, but was standing up in the *prie-dieu*; she turned her back to the altar, bent forward, then furtively looked round at him again. In her dress the woman did not greatly differ from the other, who must have departed with an almost incredible swiftness and stealth. The new one was dressed in the same dark, unassuming colours—Andreas, on the way, had seen the wives and daughters of the humbler townsfolk dressed thus in respectable uniformity—but this one wore no shawl. Her black hair hung in curls on both sides of her face, and her bearing was such that it was not possible to confuse her with the oppressed and grieving creature whose place she had taken so suddenly and noiselessly. There was something impudent and almost childish in the way in which she looked round angrily several times, then peeped over her shoulder to note the effect of her look. She might just as well have been trying to frighten off an intruder as to awaken curiosity in an indifferent onlooker; it even seemed to Andreas, as he now finally turned to go, as though she had signalled to him behind his back with open arms.

He was standing in the square, a little dazzled, when someone came out of the church behind him, and brushed past him so quickly that he felt the air move. He saw one side of a pale young face, which turned sharply away from him, with flying curls which nearly touched his cheeks. The face was twitching, as if with suppressed laughter. The swift, almost running steps, the abruptly averted face as she brushed past him—all this was too violent not to be intentional, yet it looked rather like the mischief of a child than the insolence of a grown-up. Yet the figure was that of a grown woman, and the audacious freedom of the body was so strange, as she ran towards the bridge in front of Andreas, flinging her slender legs till her skirts flew, that for a moment Andreas thought it might be some youth in disguise playing a prank on him, the obvious foreigner. And yet again, something told him unmistakably that the being before him was a girl or woman, as she herself came to a standstill on the little bridge as if waiting

for him. In the face, which he thought pretty
enough, there was a dash of impudence; the whole
behaviour looked absolutely wanton, yet there was
something about it which attracted rather than
repelled him. He did not wish to meet the young
woman on the bridge: there was no other way back
into the street. So he swung round again, mounted
the steps into the church, thinking that having now
given the woman a definite sign of refusal, he would
be rid of her. He found it strange enough that the
other woman was no longer in the church. He went
right up to the altar, glanced into the little chapels
right and left, looked behind the columns—nowhere
a trace. It was if the stone floor had opened and
swallowed up the mourner, casting up in her place
that other strange creature.

When Andreas again emerged onto the square, he
saw, to his relief, that the bridge was clear. He went
back into the street, wondering whether he had not,
after all, missed Zorzi coming out, and whether Zorzi
might have gone to look for him in the direction they
had come from. A clean-looking house next door to
the one with the brass knocker now seemed to him to
be the right one, because the door was standing open.
He went in, meaning to knock at some door on the
ground floor, ask for Nina, then go up himself and
discover the artist's whereabouts. He did so all the

more quickly since he imagined that from about the second house after he had crossed the bridge, a light footfall and a swish of skirts had dogged his steps. From the entrance hall the stairs led upwards, but Andreas turned aside and went into the courtyard to look for a porter's lodge or some other human dwelling. The courtyard was small, enclosed by walls, quite overgrown with vine-leaves to a considerable height: the loveliest ripe grapes of a reddish kind hung down into it, strong wooden posts supported the living roof; there was a nail driven into one of them with a bird-cage hanging on it. At one point in the vine-leaf roof there was a gap, big enough for a child to climb through. From that point the glow of the radiant sky above fell into the courtyard, and the beautiful shapes of the vine-leaves were sharply outlined on the tiled floor. This not very big place, half room, half garden, was filled with pleasant warmth and the scent of grapes, and silence so deep that Andreas could hear the restless movements of the bird which, untroubled by his approach, hopped from perch to perch.

Suddenly the careless bird dashed itself in terror against the side of its cage, the beams of the vine-roof rocked, the opening darkened abruptly, and over Andreas's head, at the height of a man, a human face looked in. Black eyes, with whites glittering in contrast, fixed his startled gaze from above, a

mouth half open with strain and excitement, dark
curls on one side slid down among grapes. The
whole pale face was wild and tense, with a flash of
satisfaction, almost childishly unconcealed. The body
lay somehow on the light trellis of the roof, the feet
were most likely hanging in a hook in the wall, the
finger-tips on the top of a post. Then a mysterious
change came over the expression of the face. With
infinite sympathy, even love, the eyes rested on
Andreas. One hand forced its way through the
leaves, as if to reach his head, to stroke his hair, the
four fingers were bleeding at the tips. The hand did
not reach Andreas, a drop of blood fell on his forehead, the face above him turned white. "I'm falling,"
cried the mouth… one moment had been the reward
of unspeakable effort. The pale face was wrenched
away, the light body jerked upwards, then slid back
over the wall. How it reached the ground on the
other side Andreas could no longer hear; he was
running to the front of the house to cut off the mysterious being's retreat. It could only be the house on
the right; either she would come out of it, or she had
jumped down into the courtyard and must be hiding
there. He stood in front of the house door—it was
the one with the dolphin. It was shut and did not
yield to his pressure.

He had already raised the knocker, when he

thought he heard steps approaching within. His heart was beating so that those inside must hear it. Hardly ever in his life had he been in such a state; for the first time the inexplicable, a departure from any conceivable order, had singled him out, he felt that the secret would never let him rest: he saw the girl climbing up the naked walls, wrenching herself upwards by the crevices to reach him; he saw her, with bleeding hands, crouching in a corner of the courtyard, trying to escape him. His thoughts went no further: a rapid step approaching the door half robbed him of his senses. The door opened. Zorzi stood before him.

"For God's sake, tell me who it was!" cried Andreas, and before Zorzi could answer, before he could ask, ran past him to the end of the passage.

"Where are you going?" Zorzi asked him.

"Into the courtyard—let me go."

"The house has no courtyard: there's a blank wall here, with the canal behind it and the garden of the Redentore monastery beyond."

Andreas could not understand a word. He had lost all sense of direction; he told his story, and saw that he could tell nothing, that he had not the power to tell how momentous was the experience he had lived through.

"Whoever the person is," said Zorzi, "rest assured

that if she ever shows herself in this quarter again, I shall find out who she is: she won't escape me, whether she is a man in disguise or a street woman having some fun."

Andreas knew only too well that neither the one nor the other was anywhere near the truth. He could understand nothing, yet, in his heart of hearts, rejected any explanation. How gladly would he have hurried back into the church, to find, if not his mysterious enemy and friend, the nameless, strange woman who climbed up walls to swoop down on her prey from above—then at the very least her companion; for now it seemed impossible that the two beings, one of whom had risen in the other's place, like the glass of red and yellow wine in the hand of the conjurer, should be ignorant of each other. He could not imagine why he had not thought of the connection before. He felt how careless his search of the church has been; he ought to have been able to find a trace—a crack in a wall—a secret door. If only he had been alone, how eagerly he would have hurried back! The imperious need to seek and find would have urged him back again, and then again, a third and fourth time. It had often happened so: a letter mislaid—a key we know we have; but Zorzi would not let him go. "Leave your climbing manwoman—you'll see more than that in Venice—and hurry up to Nina. She's expecting you. I can't tell you all that's been going on up there again. The Duke of Camposagrado, her protector, in a fit of rage and jealousy, stuck a rare singing-bird she had had sent to her by a Jewish admirer, Signor dalle Torre, into his mouth, living, and bit its head off. Then he was suspicious about the Hungarian captain and Nina, and had him thrashed half out of his life, and what's more he seems to have got hold of the wrong man, and now the *sbirri* are after him, and have searched her lodgings. In fact, everything is upside-down, and that's just the moment for a newcomer to get into her good graces."

Andreas was only half listening. The staircase was narrow and dark; he hoped at every turn in it to see the strange woman appear, and even at the top, in front of Nina's door, he half expected her to flit by. It now seemed beyond the possibility of doubt that a secret connection had existed between the two gestures—the imploring gesture of the mourner had been meant for him, just like the signal of the young girl. His excitement, his impatience to unravel the mystery of this being, was hardly bearable; she had, in some incomprehensible fashion, found the way to be alone with him for an instant: a high wall, perhaps with water flowing below it, had not deterred her from doing what seemed impossible to any creature but a cat: the blood flowing from her fingers had not daunted her. She would find the way to him again, always, everywhere.

They found Signorina Nina on a sofa in a very easy, very pretty posture. Everything about her was light, and of a most charming, delicate plumpness. Her hair was as fair as bleached gold, and she wore it unpowdered. Three things, which were charmingly curved, and perfectly in keeping, her eyebrows, her mouth, and her hand, were raised to greet the entering guest with an expression of quiet curiosity and great friendliness.

An unframed picture was leaning with its face to the wall. There was a gash through the canvas, as though it had been slashed by a knife. Zorzi picked it up and looked at it, shaking his head. "What do you think of the likeness?" he said, holding out the portrait to Andreas, who had sat down on a stool at Nina's feet. The portrait was such that a coarse eye would have been struck by the likeness. Nina's features were there, but they looked cold and mean. In reality, her brows, with their faint upward curve, were charming because they were traced on a face which was almost too soft; a severe judge would have found her neck not slender enough, but in the set of the head on the neck there was something enchantingly helpless and womanly. In the portrait the curve of the eyebrows was vulgar in its emphasis, the neck, cut through by the knife, was fleshy and lascivious. The eyes were fixed on the beholder with cold, insolent fire. It was one of those painful portraits of which it can be said that they contain the inventory of a face, but reveal the soul of the artist. Andreas felt a wave of inward aversion.

"Take it out of my sight," said Nina. "It means nothing but annoyance and brutality to me."

"I shall mend this one," said Zorzi, "and paint another, only this time on a Flemish, not a Venetian, ground. It will be still better, and I shall make both the gentlemen pay twice. I should be an ass if I could not manage to make them both pay me."

"Well, what do you think of it?" she asked, when the artist had vanished with his production.

"I think it is a very good likeness and very ugly."

"That's a pretty compliment."

He made no answer.

"Now you have been with me for not more than a minute and have already said something unkind. Do you think too that men are given greater strength and sharper wits and a louder voice just to make life harder for us poor women?"

"I don't mean it in that way," Andreas hastened to say. "If I were to paint you the picture would turn out quite differently, you may be sure."

He said so much, and would have liked to say a great deal more, for she seemed unspeakably charming. But the thought that Zorzi might come back into the room at any moment disturbed him, and he said no more. Perhaps he had said enough—he did not know—for it is not words that matter, but a tone of voice—a look.

Nina looked, as if absently, past him; on her upper lip, which was curved like her eyebrows, and seemed as if it were ready to yield to something that was to come, there hovered the shadow of a smile—it seemed to be waiting for a kiss. Without thinking Andreas bent forward, a little dazed, looking at the half-open lips. Romana rose before him, only to vanish into air. He felt as if something delicious, yet intimidating, was settling softly on his heart, to dissolve there.

"We are alone now," he said, "but who knows for how long?" He stretched out his hand for hers, yet did not take it, for he seemed to feel Zorzi's hand on the door-handle. Andreas stood up and went to the window.

Andreas looked through the window and saw below him a pretty little roof-garden. On a flat terrace orange trees stood in tubs, lillies and roses grew out of wooden boxes, and ramblers formed a walk and a little arbour. A fig tree in the middle even bore a few ripe figs.

He asked: "Does the garden belong to you?"

"It doesn't belong to me, and I should like so much to rent it," returned Nina, "but I can't pay those greedy people what they want. If I had it I should have a basin made with a little fountain in it—Zorzi says it could be done—and have a lamp put in the arbour."

Andreas saw himself going into the neighbour's house, paying the rent down on the table—then he saw himself coming back to Signorina Nina with the lease. In imagination he was already giving orders for the trellis round the roof-garden to be raised: climbing roses and convolvulus were winding up the slender lattice-work, turning the little space into a living-room, with the stars looking in from above. The night breeze played through it, the inquisitive looks of the neighbours were shut out. Fruit stood in dishes on little tables, among lights under glass shades: Nina was lying on a sofa in a light wrap, much as she lay before him in reality. But what a different Andreas stood before her! Dreamily he felt that other self: he was no chance visitor, to whom a vague, absent-minded quarter of an hour was granted. He was the legitimate lover, the master of the enchanted garden, the master of his mistress. He was lost in a vague sense of happiness, as though the sound of an Aeolian harp were pulsing through him. He did not know how little need there was of all these schemes, that the very next moment might have meant happiness.

"What is it?" asked Nina, and in her voice there lay the expression of faint wonder that came so naturally to her.

Her voice recalled him to himself. It occurred to him that it must be possible to look down from the roof-garden on to that roof of vine-leaves which stretched from one blank wall to the other and on to the canal which flowed between that courtyard and the garden of the Redentore monastery. The thought of his unknown came to him, but with terror. That being was in the world—here was something from which he could never escape. His breast contracted, he felt as if he must seek a refuge. He turned back into the room, and, leaning on the back of the sofa, bent over Nina. Her upper lip, which was delicately arched, like her eyebrows, was raised in slight wonder.

"I was thinking that I am living in the rooms where you used to live, and that I am living there alone," he said, but his words came heavily. "If you had the little garden down there, and the arbour with the lamp in it, I should be glad to live there with somebody—really glad—but not with the one that man carried away. I should not like to live with her in any house, in any arbour, on any island. And you have no arbour, and no lamp in it!"

He would have liked to kneel before her, to lay his head in her lap; but he said all this, and especially the last sentence, in a cold, almost gloomy tone, for he thought that a woman must divine all that was going on in him. In speaking with this hard sarcasm of the Nina of the picture, she must know that another Nina was closer to him, and he to her, than could ever be said in words, and that his whole being was ready to create the circumstances whose non-existence he emphasized so caustically. But at the same moment a strange, sad picture rose before him—it was the memory of childish dreams, which seemed now far remote, and had been repeated *ad nauseam*: he had crept hungry to the pantry to cut himself a piece of bread; he had pressed the loaf to him, knife in hand, but again and again had cut past the loaf into the void.

His hand, without boldness, without hope even, had taken Nina's hand, which was charming without being thin, and delicate without being small. She yielded it to him, he even thought he felt the fingers close about his with a soft, steady pressure. Her look was veiled, and the depths of her blue eyes seemed to darken; the hint of a smile still lay on her upper lip, but a fading, almost anxious smile that seemed to call for a kiss. Nothing could have startled him more deeply than such signs, which would have made another bold, even insolent. He was utterly dazed. How could he grasp what was so simple and so near? He did not think of the woman over whom he was leaning, but in a lightning flash he saw her mother, her father, her sister, her brothers, he saw the choleric duke rise from the space round the sofa, the bleeding head of a parrot in his hand; the head of a Jewish admirer pushed its noiseless way beside him—he looked like the servant, but wore no wig; and the Hungarian captain, whose hair was in plaits, ferociously brandished a curved knife.

He wondered if all the ready money he possessed would be enough to release Nina from all these phantoms, and had to admit, for a week perhaps, for three days. And what good was a single gift, even if it was going to beggar him, when, it seemed to him, decency demanded that he should provide an income, perhaps even a lodging, a house, newly furnished, and servants—at least, he reflected, a maid and a manservant? Gotthilff's face leered up at him; the beauty of the moment dissolved. He felt he must let go of Nina's hand; he did so with a gentle pressure. She looked at him; again something like wonder was mingled with her expression, yet it was cooler than before. He had taken his leave, he did not know how, and had asked permission to return.

Downstairs he found Zorzi, who had the picture, wrapped up in paper, under his arm, and seemed to be waiting for him. He dismissed him quickly. He repented bitterly of having spoken to the man of his unknown; he was glad that Zorzi did not begin to speak of her. For nothing in the world ought he to have put on her track just the man whose eyes seemed to be spying on him and everybody else. He told him that he would soon visit Signorina Nina again, and did not believe it himself. Hardly had Zorzi departed with his picture when he was on his way through the street; under the archway, over the bridge, to the church.

The square lay deserted as before: the empty boat hung motionless below the bridge. It looked to Andreas like a sign of encouragement. He walked as if in a dream and did not really doubt—had no other thought than that the mourner would be sitting there, and would raise her arms anxiously, imploringly, towards him as he entered. Then he would withdraw, knowing that behind his back the other would rise from the same *prie-dieu* to follow him. This mystery was not past for him, but something that was repeated in the form of a circle, and he only had to step back into the circle to restore it to the present.

He entered the church—it was empty. He returned to the square, stood on the bridge, looked in every house, and found nobody. He went away, wandered through a few streets, then after a time returned to the square and entered the church through the side door, went back through the archway, and found nobody.

JOURNAL OF HERR VON N'S
TOUR TO VENICE, 1779

I REMEMBER things very exactly—always had a good memory, won the Grand Cross of Excellence at school because I could recite the rulers of Austria forwards and backwards. I also took note of all my mother's servants, and all my grandfather's minerals, and the names of the stars in Orion.

Reasons for the tour to Venice: Artists, great names. Palaces, behaviour in drawing-rooms, starting a conversation. To make an appearance, to please. What I already knew about Venice: Uncle had friend whose relatives had been cast into *oubliettes* (with nails and razors)...

Arrival: Early morning. Hungry. Chilly. Starts out to look for lodgings. Troop of actors waiting on canal bank. An actress ogles him from the lap of a fellow-actor.

Walks through a street or two. The half-naked gentleman, he has a hat with a veil of coarse lace on his arm, a fine but tattered shirt. He addresses him, says he knows Vienna, mentions names. Declares he has gambled away everything he possesses. I lend him my cloak; he speaks very nobly of generosity, of times gone by. The gentleman tells how he took a lady of fashion to Grassalkovich's; she said, *Brutto nome, pare una bestemmia* (an ugly name, it sounds like a curse), and would not have him as a lover. When he is dressed, his tone is much more sociable, less elevated.

Smell of cooking. The stranger will not let him breakfast here, promises to procure him a lodging at a nobleman's, goes with him.

The lady of the house, the nobleman, the old man. I give money for breakfast to be brought. Am given the room of the daughter, who has left home. Everybody is connected with the theatre. Groans from above: the artist has colic. We go up, the stone is removed; meanwhile the nobleman brings the little fish in his daughter's handkerchief. We eat real Venetian *frittatura*.

Up again to the artist, he shows me the portrait of a beautiful woman (for dalle Torre), promises to take me to see her. On the way, tells the story of the Duke of Camposagrado's two pictures; when the brothers send him theirs, he laughs immoderately and assigns a sum of money for them to send him the Goya, copy the Tintorettos. Artist promises to present me to the Duke.

Arrive at the beautiful lady's. Bird in cage, fine porcelain hyacinths in front. Camposagrado. Present;

details of the Pyrenean village where the Duke is magistrate.

The young lady in the other room with him. Camposagrado very angry, devours the bird and goes. I am introduced, behave with reserve. The old woman suggests I should give a present. I withdraw, cannot take things lightly. This would be the moment for an irresponsible blackguard or a clever swindler. I invite her to supper.

Go out on to the Piazza. Miss a procession, see a patrician putting on a harlequin costume. Go to the theatre. The veiled (masked) lady. Letter received on the Piazzetta.

The Knight Sacramozo sits down beside me. His appearance. The servant with the letter. The servant seems to know the Knight. Tell the Knight that I have invited the courtesan. He is surprised that it all fits in.—Go to bed. Mosquitoes.

Next morning: appointment with the Knight. To the lady's, at her morning toilet. Am first shown into an anteroom, while the lady retires with the Knight. The lady comes, makes somewhat casual apologies. The Knight goes to breakfast with me, explains his conception of love. Former passion for the courtesan. His attempted suicide.

In the afternoon the nobleman returns to bring me my cloak, takes me to the notary.

In the evening, near Madonna dell'Orto. The beautiful lady at a window.

In the church, Camposagrado with servants to light him; returns alone, is attacked by a dog. He masters the dog with his teeth.

HERR VON N'S ADVENTURE
IN VENICE

ANDREAS: two halves which gape asunder.—
Andreas's character not yet formed: he must
first find himself in these vicissitudes. His shyness, his
pride—all untested till now.—Not clear about his
own state of mind—always too much, too little.
Doubts whether he really committed the crime on
the dog.

Andreas: main line, courage—the courage incorporated in the air of Venice, courage in the night of
storm. Morality: courage.

Tour due to the calculating *snobisme* of his father.

How Andreas imagines the life of great gentlemen
(from the tales of the lackey, his grandfather, from
his own experiences too). From the stag-rutting into
the castle, changes clothes, hair dressed, calls for a
mistress to take her to the opera *Armida*.

Andreas (if he goes to the bottom of it) goes to
Venice chiefly because the people there are always
masked. After the adventure in the country with the
haughty Countess, who had treated him like a
lackey, the idea, half-dreamed, had taken shape in

his mind that the adventure would have been glorious if he had been masked. In a general way he is now haunted by the difference between being and seeming—for instance, when he sees haycocks which look like countrywomen in hats or like monks, and which give him an eerie and solemn feeling, and are really senseless things.

Chapters (provisional): I. Castle Finazzer. II. Arrival. III. Three New Friends. IV. The Knight of Malta. V. Double Life. VI. A Conversation. VII. The Demonic. VIII. Departure.

Chapter I. The end. The mountains:—he has no wish to live there; at this moment he is richer than the mountaineer, richer than the mountain-dweller; he feels no need to relate things to Romana—it is entirely self-enjoyment, but possible only through her. When he had that—it was the pledge that he would possess Romana too.

Camposagrado: a thick-set man, with a pearl drop in one ear containing a fragment of the Host.

CHAPTER V. The New Friend (The Knight of Malta).

Andreas had fallen into an unpleasant state of mind. The thought of home poisoned the "here": the "here" made him think more sadly of home.

He delivered the letter and was told that the master

was dead. The business friend gone away. He asked
for his trunk, a sign that he was longing for news
from home. The bread tastes stale. He misses the
coaches, the elegance; the people mean so little,
compared with the Graben and the Kohlmarkt. A
lady descending from her equipage in Vienna.

He tries to see Nina, without any real hope. (Zorzi
tells him that the Knight wants to know his name;
asks whether he needs anything. Andreas declines.)
He dislikes the part of him that wants to go to her.
He is not received.

Evening. Talk with Zustina on the staircase. He
asks her why she does not wish to marry. How could
she suspect that he was speaking of himself? She
rebuffs him. Her justification: "They are gentlemen:
there is good in every one of them. The mother of a
simpleton has taken a ticket for him." He, jealous of
happy people. He tells her that he is probably leaving Venice. She is unmoved.—Her picture of the
world: family tyrants or gamblers of all kinds. She
removes herself from him.

Various visits to Nina, a second time two days
later, a third—but always obstacles. Once somebody
is with her, another time "out," or "ill"—once he is
shown in and hears her in the next room, but "she
has had to go out." Yet he is always encouraged to
return.—The situation becomes quite inexplicable

when Zustina says to him: "Nina is so sorry that you are neglecting her."—Feeling of helplessness.

Sights of the town. A trial. Processions. Jesuits. Churches. Pictures: Tintoretto: distinction, boldness, self-confidence.

Envy of all human beings, hypochondria, growing distaste for people. Too many people, would have liked to sweep them all away from him. Longing for trees (to embrace a tree). Gazing towards the mountains. Recollection of that moment. Melancholy. His thoughts become more disorderly and impure.

Sea-monster for ten *soldi* from Crete, peculiar interior. To fill the void in him, goes not to the church but to the booth. The Spanish woman (the mask).

The merman: "What a spectacle—but alas! only a spectacle!"—gives him all that the theatre did not give him, although an animal, and hardly a real one. Pain that the merman should impress him more than the real theatre.

The mask. Her arm rests on his. The mask speaks tenderly. "Our first meeting was a great day for me. I had just arrived from a dreadful place; your face was the first—I could not but love it. I was free for anything, would have liked to swoop down from above, sure that I could fly. Have you any idea of what it means to be a prisoner?" (he thinks of the lead roofs).

He doubts. She: "What I say is real—cannot you feel it?" (the pressure of her hand). He assures her that when he was with Nina that time, he thought of nothing but her. "And on your later visits?"

The mask speaks tenderly; she speaks of Nina—he puts things together: "It is she." The blood surges to his heart.

The mask: "I *forced* a certain person to ask your name. There is a lifetime between that day and this."

Andreas resolves to put various questions to Zustina in order to find out the truth about his unknown. Again does nothing. It means too much effort.

In the house: "Your friend was asking for you"—a vine-leaf with a drop of blood on it.

Lonelier here among people than there on the dog's grave.

A mask wishes to take him to gaming-rooms. He refuses, turns back in the anteroom, asks her to tell him at any rate who she is and where she is going to take him. The mask has told him that there are various people interested in him besides the Knight. (Two persons at least. How does she know?) On the staircase, he thinks he recognizes the young Spanish woman, or another young person from Nina's house. (She knows too about his visits to Nina.)

119

Enters a church, hopes to see the Spanish woman. Is rapt into a dreamlike height, but only for a moment. There is somebody kneeling behind him, sighing, like a being at his mercy. This person leans against the edge of the step—looks into the distance.

THE NEXT day to the Dogana. Letter about the condition of the Empress. Discomfort. The whole world so dreadfully puppet-like.

Somebody follows him in a gondola, catches up with him: the Knight, who says he has been looking for him in the little coffee-house. A letter, similar to the first, has been thrown into the Knight's house. "Do you really know nothing about it? Might I ask you to go over in your mind the people you have met in society? Nothing stands alone: everything is fulfilled in circles. Much escapes us, and yet it is in us, and all we need to know is how to bring it to the surface. Somebody I am deeply devoted to is greatly distressed by this affair. I will tell you what was in the letter. Have you any relatives in Italy?" (*Fluidum* of kinship).

Andreas: "I should like to tell you so much about myself that your suspicions would be disarmed."— Strange lack of self-confidence that his word does not seem to suffice even to himself! At the same time, mortal fear that, once the suspicion is removed, the Knight will lose all interest in him. How happy he felt when the man was sitting by him! Wonder that even this man should suffer some secret torment.

Pleasant stroll afterwards. Knight: "Do not miss going to Murano—you hear the best music there. Your ambassador often goes there too."

Meanwhile a one-armed messenger brings a letter for Andreas. "Who is it from?"—"Your Honour knows." Knight wonders at the coincidence. He asks the Knight to go with him. The Knight refuses. Is piqued—assumes that Andreas was laughing at him. "You receive the messenger I was telling you about."

FIRST SIGHT of the Knight. Intimation of harmonious contrast between appearance and spirit. Something witty about him that is simply that contrast.

At the beginning, Andreas's chief objection to the Knight: the casualness of the acquaintance. "He cannot be worth much, since he had time to spend with me."

The hours with Sacramozo were the radiance in his day. How astonished he was when Sacramozo spoke to him! Then he was annoyed, because it made the Knight seem ordinary.

How the Knight, in his eyes, always grows in beauty out of his ugliness, and he gradually comes to feel that the essence of the man is all love, or all form. His double nature: when he speaks on mystic subjects (for him, given the right connections, everything in the world, even the most commonplace circumstances and doings, can be included in them) he is candid, accessible to union, merely human, communicative of himself, accessible by enthusiasm.

When he is in ordinary surroundings, he is completely set apart by courtesy; inconceivable that he could be touched, influenced, reached. It is impossible, when he is in this state, to attempt to remind him of the other. Here he exercises a power which is as coercive as the other is persuasive. Sometimes, in his worldly aloofness, he seems still stranger to Andreas: the idea "the power of despair" to be applied to him in this situation.

Meetings with the Knight. The only being able to concentrate him: at the same time bewilders him: by being at home in the world: by his discretion, his acceptance of everything as a matter of course—Andreas's fear in imperfect moments: that everything in Sacramozo may be merely show.

The Knight does not invite him home; seems to take for granted that he has friends, that he knows where the pictures are to be seen, etc.

The essence of his being: the secrets; alludes to them by *minus dicere*, not by *plus dicere*. The essence of his being a knowledge of the mystery of how man is organized.

CONVERSATIONS with Sacramozo:

Andreas full of prejudices; the worst against himself; his money prejudices, his prejudices as regards the world—as regards himself: thinks he has thrown away his happiness, everything is deteriorating, everything is stale. Sacramozo:

"You are rich in hidden powers.—You exclude the extraordinary—you are wrong. You speak of happiness. How could you enjoy it? Ask rather—*who* is it that enjoys it?"

Sacramozo teaches him to realize the function of poetry through Ariosto: poetry is not concerned with nature. The poet is a poet by virtue of his penetration *of* nature (of life).

As to Ariosto: the true domain of poetry is the impossible (the youth whose body moved through his armour).

Poetry as the present. The mystic element in poetry: the conquest of time.—

It is in the transitions that we recognize the sublime. All life is a transition.

In all our doings we must follow examples: there lies the grandeur of Christianity.—Unspiritual Christians cheat God: dirt behind the altar.—

To know our element: we really live only under the eyes of one who loves us. Sacramozo: "Attention means as much as love. I beg you to treat my soul with attention. Who is attentive? The diplomat, the official, the doctor, the priest... not one attentive enough. The statement 'I have neglected nothing'—who can pronounce it of himself with a clear conscience?"

What we truly participate in, to that we are already half united. Sacramozo on the participation of negroes in their masters' pleasure: he has found what he sought—he has received a letter.

Sacramozo explains the repulsion of the soul for what it has recently experienced.

How far a man like Sacramozo has outgrown all fears, yet all terrors are near him, to be called up at the slightest touch: what fear, terror, timidity mean.

How far, for Sacramozo, all material is material for the divine.—Andreas broods: "Why with me, of all people?"—(Andreas must overcome that.) Sacramozo: "Everything is everywhere, but only for the moment."

To be able to ask somebody's pardon—how far this means a higher understanding has been reached.

All that a man like Sacramozo is henceforth incapable of—there lies his grandeur.

Sacramozo objects to the expression "to go deeper into things"—it should be replaced by "to become aware"—"to remember."

Spirit is of *one essence*. In the spiritual world, there are no stages, only degrees of penetration. Spirit is action, perfect or less perfect. At some point you are preventing the world from thinking. Human beings are the sufferings and acts of the spirit.

Through Sacramozo, Andreas realizes that he loves Romana Finazzer.

Sacramozo believes in the twofold. Thus he tells the two determining experiences of his life. "It takes a man of natural genius (like Francis of Assisi) to be determined for ever by a single experience. The ordinary human being, when his way is cut off in one direction by some dreadful experience, will move in the other."—As a rule, too, we create an individual out of a type by crossing it with another species: Narcisse is a rogue, but a respectable musician (cf. Goethe's *Note*).

Knight: "You often mention your uncle in a peculiar way—he must mean a great deal to you" (more encouragement from Sacramozo inconceivable). Andreas blushed. The story of Uncle Leopold and the two momentous days. Beside the death-bed: the widow, the second family—peasant lads.—The della Spina: "We have both lost so much, dear lady."—While Andreas is speaking, Castle Finazzer, that day of gloom, comes back to him. The Knight (with a warm-hearted look): "You told that beautifully."

The human is nobly contained in him, and is beautifully detached.—He proposes a visit.

Chapter VI. A Visit.

"Who knows his own element?"

By the company of the Knight of Malta, by but a single allusion to him, Andreas's existence is refined and concentrated. If he meets him, he can be sure that something remarkable or at least unexpected will happen to him afterwards. His senses grow keener, he feels more capable of enjoying the individual in others. Feels himself in a greater and higher sense an individual. Love and hate are closer to him. He feels the constituent elements of his own being grow more interesting to himself, has the presentiment of beauty behind them. He feels the Knight's mastery in the playing of his own part. There is no situation in which he could not imagine him. In the Knight, he encounters supreme receptiveness for identity.

He tells himself all this, though in morbid self-reproaches. What kind of man am I for the first man of any distinction I meet to make such an impression on me?"

Beginning. The Knight catches him up on the Riva dei Schiavoni. "What a good thing I have met you." (A vague impulse has sent Andreas there.) "I nearly sent for you. You are wanted..."

Secret about Maria. At Andreas's first visit she makes a tiny, helpless gesture towards a dark corner behind her sofa with a certain stiffness about her waist—and at that moment, Andreas has a presentiment that here is an insoluble mystery, that he will never know this woman, and feels that the infinite has wounded him more violently than any definite pain that he has ever known: he has three or four memories which all bear within them this *pointe acérée de l'infini* (the spearhead of the infinite) (the meeting with the old woman and the child on that first morning)—feels this unfelt pain without realizing that, at that very moment, he *loves*.

At his first visit, Maria says, "*Somebody* will write to you again." Once he receives from Maria a letter that is passionate, almost cynical. He hurries to her; she is not at home. Later, he finds her. She is in great distress: "I have been told about the letter"— she has to bring herself to something like a confession—"my hand is bewitched: it acts against my will. I would like to cut it off, but the fifth commandment forbids that . . ." (Problem: how far am I responsible for my hand?)

Elegance and distinction, the phantoms Andreas has pursued, are embodied in Maria in their most perfect form, as nobility of the soul. He now sees the Viennese countesses as mere marionettes, worked by their breeding.

Sacramozo's relationship to Maria is this: that he

wants to amuse her in order to keep her alive, because she alone makes life worth living for him
(however little, for that matter, he demands or
expects from her).

Sacramozo has for Maria "religion, not love"
(Novalis).—The Knight: "I found her in Genoa.
Wicked people declared they had a right to her. I
protected her—and managed to bring her here. But
I mean no more to her on that account than you do.
I look upon every day as the last. Day by day, I
think, 'She will escape you!'—Andreas: "Do you
think she will enter a convent?"—Knight: "She
nearly did. But she seems to have abandoned the
idea. She told me she had received letters which dis-
suaded her."

Maria married to a wicked man at thirteen. She is
a widow: her husband was cruel. The religious crisis
which caused the split in her. A prayer (Sacramozo
tells Andreas this)—Maria regards it as a punishment for having implored Christ to be her accom-
plice in her love-affair, and thus having been guilty
of blasphemy. Since then, Maria filled with disgust
for the act itself: she feels the vague fatigue, has a
physical knowledge of the thing which appals her.

At a remark, a mere piece of news, her astral
body, consisting of her thoughts, fears, aspirations, is
often, with immense sensibility, touched by a "silent

fall of distant stars"—she feels this whole as her "I": this whole must become blessed, this whole would never have been capable of surrendering in love, this whole Andreas can never embrace, this whole is her burden and her suffering.

A midway aspect of Maria—in which the *lady* is uppermost: that all is not yet united in her, that she is neither resigned nor exhausted, that the possibilities of dying a martyr's death or petrifying in aristocratic *morgue* still lie open to her.

Sacramozo knows from confidences that Maria at times loses her identity. Sacramozo surmises as to her condition.

THE LADY (Maria) and the cocotte (Mariquita) are both Spanish: they are dissociated aspects of one and the same personality, which play *trucs* on each other. The cocotte writes Andreas the letters. The cocotte hates Sacramozo and all his sentimental fuss. Once, Andreas encounters the cocotte as he is taking leave of the lady: once, the kind lady is transformed before the mirror into the malicious cocotte. The cocotte fears Sacramozo, believes he has the evil eye (she fears, too, that he might kill her, and he actually pursues her with a knife).—The cocotte sleeps with him, this makes Andreas fall more deeply in love with the lady; he can no longer understand

Sacramozo's Platonism. In the early morning the bed is empty, he hears moans, and, with gestures of appalling distress, the *other* takes flight. During this troubled time, he once finds in his valise the fichu of the Finazzer girl.—The cocotte declares that she has to go to a rich old man.

(Portrait of Maria and Mariquita in the journal) To be with Maria is to pursue the most subtle and profound conception of the individual: Maria's religious aestheticism tends in this direction. Her chief concern is the unity, the uniqueness of the soul (but she is thwarted by the body). It would be impossible to pay her a compliment on her beauty or a detail of her figure. She declares that no tree, no cloud, has its like. She has a horror of love, whose instrument is the quid pro quo. (She brings to mind the Princess in Tasso.)

In Mariquita, it is each physical detail that seems unique and immortal—knee, hip, smile. Beyond that, she does not trouble her head much about uniqueness, she does not believe in the immortality of the soul. Her conversation, arguments, even her thoughts are all pantomime, all latent eroticism, not a word is meant for more than the moment—she perpetually courts caresses from everything around her.

The link between Maria and Mariquita is a small,

asthmatic King Charles's spaniel, Fidèle by name, a suspicious and disdainful animal which, save on *one* occasion, is always hidden in Maria's house—again the fundamental problem of *Gestern (Yesterday)*: faith, constancy, and change—Maria dimly suspects the chaos within her; that is what she has in common with Mariquita. Thus they have the spaniel in common.

ad Maria *et* Mariquita: the Franciscan father's views on the case: the views of the physician, materialistic (La Mettrie, Condillac). The anecdote of the man who was driven mad by one accident and restored by another.—"What conclusion do you draw from that?" asked the Knight.

MARIA always in mittens, hands always cold: Mariquita's hands always as if suffused with liquid, gentle fire.

Unrestraint the essence of Mariquita: constraint the essence of the Countess. The Countess speaks of the hundred-weight-heavy chains with which heaven tries its own. We are responsible for more than ourselves. The constraint in the Countess's love-letters.

With Maria, Andreas learns the value of inward freedom; with Mariquita, he feels a horror of absolute freedom. With Mariquita, he cannot but crave for the universal bond of union; with Maria, for the universal solvent: thus his nature must be revealed to him.

Maria is marvellously well dressed, Mariquita likes dirt and disorder.

Maria can hardly endure the scent of flowers; one day, Andreas finds her half fainting, surrounded by strongly scented flowers: Mariquita has bought the flowers at market that morning and sent them to Maria by a Friuli man.

Maria is a Christian, with mystic, Molinistic leanings; Sacramozo is indifferent; Mariquita is a pagan, she believes in the moment and in nothing else.

What Mariquita thinks of Maria (in letters or monologues, from time to time): she hates her, sees all her imperfections, thinks her a *coward* (just as Michelangelo thinks himself a coward in contrast to Savonarola), yet she is her most personal theme, the only one that interests her. She envies her her distinction, without being quite aware of what that distinction is, what it is that lends to Maria's every action a royal, immaterial worth (like the horn on the brow of the unicorn, like a tower in the moon); she even tries to make Maria herself suspicious of this privilege, to submerge her in meanness (though she would be the one to suffer most by it)—she writes to her: "your dream of yesterday, that there is no such thing as the common, that it can all be overcome, that life could be lived in a perpetual *élan*, with none of your crouching in a corner—is a projection of your fathomless vanity, of your stupid incapacity to face reality."

Mariquita's stories (of Maria): sometimes as if she were an old hag, then: "that must be taken metaphorically. People must always be taken metaphorically. She is quite a pretty woman, but a fiend all the same. That is why she wants people to think her an angel: but, no woman in the world is seen through as I see through her. My eyes go beneath the skin."

MARIQUITA: the various aspects of the demonic: mischievous, quick-witted, cynical, restless, godless. Shameless, libertine, dread of churches. Boundlessly inquisitive. Brilliant, *ingénue*. Utterly forgetful.

The element connecting all her phases—a kind of puppet-like activity. She must have something going on: she hates repose, meditation—for then she is afraid of being dissolved in the other.

Once Mariquita breaks out to the duenna (Andreas pretends to be asleep): "Curse her! She would like to lock me up in a convent because I am growing too much for her! I'll have to set him at her a bit."— Duenna: "Couldn't you give her something to make her disappear for good?"— Mariquita: "She has a hideous strength, not only when she is praying, but at other times—a kind of inward elevation which makes me feel as if I were going to be sick; I am quite weak compared to her."—Duenna: "Couldn't you contrive to make one of your best poses occur to her while she is praying?"—Mariquita: "Then she feels me coming and holds me down, those are my nastiest moments. Then I hate as the man in hell must hate God."

(Mariquita only understands her relationship to Maria bit by bit; at first, she hopes quite soon to free herself.)

Scene where Mariquita, in great distress because Maria wants to enter a convent, tells Andreas to seduce Maria; her uncanny, cringing look in this scene. In Andreas's suspicion that the old crone has something to do with experiments of the kind which led to the "Moreau horrors," that she may be providing material for an experimenter of this kind.

In trying to awaken the soul in Mariquita, Andreas endangers Mariquita's life (her separate existence): she hints anxiously at this. Thus she takes him into her arms and with tears in her eyes declares she is ready to sacrifice herself to the happiness he might find with another. He feels that she is really in earnest.

Mariquita demonic to the verge of sorcery. Succubus. Once she sleeps with two men at the same time; she says: "Suppose I had slept with the one a day, six hours, two hours, half an hour, ten minutes after the other—well what then?"

Mariquita hates the idea of "truth." "If only I never had to hear the silly word—if only you would leave me in peace with your philosophy—since the world is, after all, 'consummable, so to speak.'"

Her gloomy image of the Knight. The pattern of his life fills her with horror. When she speaks of him, she turns pale.

Mariquita never writes, only sends messages by word of mouth; writing only exists to complicate and compromise everything.

Mariquita's lodging: two rooms in a ramshackle palace, in the utmost disorder. The duenna, the old crone, lives in a large room behind. The bright room, as open as an aviary, where Mariquita bathes, takes her meals, and receives her guests. A little garden outside. The rich Jewish admirer, dalle Torre. Mariquita at first treats Andreas badly, but as soon as she notices that Maria likes to see him, invites him back with an invitation full of allusions to Maria. She hopes at last to seduce Maria by means of Andreas.

On the very day on which Andreas receives the invitation, Sacramozo receives a message full of insults: she is tired of him and is going to look around for someone else.

Mariquita, on the first visit, though she treats him badly, fondles his hand, saying: "Pretty hand—a pity you belong to a cold and miserly master."

She tells him why people love him: his gravity, his reserve, nobody can tell what he will be like, nobody can be sure of having him entirely.

Mariquita—a kind of vertigo of existence. One night she goes for a drive with Andreas in the mail-coach. *Embrouilleuse*: everything goes wrong, the desperate confusion of all things—a whole concatenation of ill-planned arrangements, nothing fits in. Café in Mestre, in the carriage she is another being. Treats him as if he were a Casanova, imputes meetings with the Countess to him (complete in all psychological and realistic details), then, in the end: "Forgive me!"—then, violently: "And why not? Why don't you take her?" He tries to tear himself away from her, then she hints at a secret, promises she will soon reveal her soul.

An adventure with Mariquita in the night of storm. She tries to throw the unconscious gondolier— the gondolier stunned by a blow from Andreas—into the water.

The courtesan wants to seduce the wild man; an excursion into the country is made for the purpose.

ANDREAS's opposing feelings in the presence of the

two women: to be with Maria makes him happy, the world seems more beautiful; Mariquita makes him gloomy, tense, fierce—afterwards ill-tempered, fatigued.

It seems incomprehensible that Maria's hand should ever be seen, felt in a sensual movement. Mariquita's foot returns pressure like a hand, clings, presses, like a softer, blinder, still more sensual hand.

Andreas: his feeling for Maria growing, so that his head swims at the thought of an intimacy (—merely to lay his hand on her knee), when he thinks intensely of her womânliness. He even grows jealous of Sacramozo. By becoming very insistent, he makes it possible for Mariquita to appear.

Andreas and the idea of "elegance": elegant people are to him what Savonarola or a very aloof young nobleman were to Michelangelo. The love of the fine lady: that is his first goal; he imagines that he will be changed by it, as his grandfather was changed by the favours of the archduchess. He says to himself: "If I were her lover..."—but he cannot really imagine himself in that situation; it seems to him that he would then be a different man (for a moment, he thinks that the Knight believes him to be her lover)... gradually it dawns upon him that for him, Maria dwells in the sphere of the unattainable; he has a premonition that his fate lies here, that this is a wound whose sharpness he must always seek to allay. He suspects that Maria's love must be directed to something in him which is unattainable to himself, utterly remote from his vanity, his restlessness, his consciousness.

With Maria, Andreas is excessively shy, so perfectly does she guide the conversation. The mere thought of asking her an intimate question (for instance, whether she knows anything about the existence of her illegitimate sister) gives him the same feeling as the thought that he might touch the mystery of her body—his head swims. Maria's soul lies like a veil over her flesh.

Ultimately, his relationship to Maria is such that he is tormented by jealousy of Sacramozo's "objectless" friendship.

His astonishment that human beings of such a kind exist: they are softer and harder, uglier and more conscientious, more self-possessed as a whole, more sensitive in detail—he feels as though a new sense must be born in him to comprehend this. He begins to suspect that there is something haphazard about our senses.—He realizes that he is merely drifting, like a pig in a rising flood.

He feels how the Knight sustains and elevates him, every one of his sayings enlightens, he feels himself utterly Sacramozo's creature, but without oppression.

He does not know whether to be more astonished by the woman or the man.

LAST BOOK

What Sacramozo needs to win this woman is a lofty love of self, a religion of the self.

Sacramozo holds himself guilty of the death of someone he has loved: Mariquita says outright that he poisoned a woman.

Sacramozo believes himself responsible for the insanity of a charming young woman who now lives on like a greedy animal.

To see the "other" in her eyes—that has made him a philosopher. In exactly the same way, a strange change came over his father just before his death. Thus he comes to believe that *masks* are the distinguishing factor. In this sense, he says that neither Goldoni nor Molière has created a character in the individual.

In particular, he reproaches himself with having slept with this person when she was already a "lunatic." Would she like to have a shell which contains the voice of her dead lover? The duality in Maria's handwriting also arrives in this occasion.

At Sacramozo's: portrait of the lady with the Sternkreuz Order: Countess Welsberg (his mother). Sacramozo on the sayings of his German mother: he forbids himself to remember her: later, he will be allowed to remember her all the more completely.— Sacramozo has understood that his cousin's return is a dispensation, has learned to be an exile: at Welsberg, his lower nature would have prevailed, the higher development of his nature would have been checked.—Sacramozo wished to buy Welsberg Castle. The night he spent in the room with the Pyramid of Life painted on the wall. His thoughts often turn on the stages of life, of age. (His uncle of ninety-three).— Sacramozo takes for granted that of two dreams, the later always throws light on the earlier—thus everything that comes later always relates to everything that has gone before—in all directions.—The Welsberg dream: in the second he is governor, not recognized as such, who is guilty of everything, who had to pronounce sentence of death, etc.

Sacramozo: faith and superstition in time. In his hours of exaltation, he is convinced that he alone possesses the real key to the world, everybody else glides past the secret lock unaware—everything serves him, even a landscape seen once, a pool of dark water in the West Indies. He would be mad if he were not right. He is right in everything, even in taking Andreas to the Countess. His knowledge: he knows that the body forgets nothing (just like the macrocosm, the great body).—He knows Maria's life far better than the confessors.—Sacramozo's fate: the Key of Solomon in Hebbel's epigram. *("We believe we hold the key of Solomon in our hands, and can unlock heaven and earth with it, but it dissolves in figures, and, to our horror, we see the alphabet renew itself. Yet let us take comfort, it has in the meantime grown more august.")*

He likes the symbolism of the Rosicrucians: the use of words in an absolutely symbolic sense, so that the words spurn the world. For, he says, everything is in the soul, everything that has power to raise spirits, and the spirits that are to be raised. "Every word evokes spirits; whatever spirit calls, its like responds" (Novalis).

In this way he can grasp the essence of poetry—the magic of configurations. To him, Goldoni (Zustina's world, the utterly unmetaphysical) is abhorrent, Molière means little, the *mimus* is indifferent; the vital thing is the *incantatio*. True poetry is the arcanym that unites us with life, separates us from life. Separation— if we separate, death itself can be borne, only the impure is horrible (a fine, pure hour of death like Stilling's)—but it is as indispensable to unite as to separate—the *aurea catena* of Homer—*"Separabis terram ab igne, subtile a spisso, suaviter magna cum ingenio"* (Thou shalt separate earth from fire, the subtle from the dense, smoothly and with great skill) (*Tabula smaragdina Hermetis*).

Sacramozo knows the power of the creative function. "We know only in so far as we create. We only know creation in so far as we are ourselves God. We do not know it in so far as we are world" (Novalis). Sacramozo knows: things are simply what the power of a human soul unceasingly makes them. Unceasing creation. The relation between two human beings as a sylph born of them (Rosicrucians).

He seeks life where it is to be found: in all that is most delicate, in the folds of things.

The abyss in such a being as Sacramozo: the despair of the onlooker, who must ask: "Do I even exist? If I must go—shall I have been?—have I known hate-love?—or was it all nothing?"

What does a man like Sacramozo *want*—a raving of anger at his impotence—"His Impotenceship."

He suffers the sylph born of Andreas and the Countess, which is the stronger, to kill the weaker, whose father he is.

Sacramozo on the mystic limbs of men: it is rapture merely to think of them, to move them in silence (Maria's dream).

On Powers: the man who is capable of prayer: "If the Countess could pray, she would be healed."

Sacramozo's mystic love of children, human beings as such, neither man nor woman, but both in one.

Andreas has to learn from the Knight: to discern

142

what has real existence, to overcome the mean and common (—everything Austrian is mean and common, the hordes of chamberlains, everything in masses. In Vienna, the chief concern of everybody is to be taken for somebody).

Sacramozo's pessimistic conception: whether I am a Christian or an atheist, a fatalist or a sceptic—I shall decide that as soon as I know who I am, where I am, and where I cease to be.

Sacramozo: "The hope and desire of man to return to his former condition is like the desire of the moth for the light" (Leonardo).

The look he fixes on the friends of his youth. Women amuse him more than men, men touch him more deeply.

Sacramozo—that is his offence—believes it is possible to lead a second life, in which everything left undone can be done, every failure made good.— "Forty years—I have nothing more to gain, but I must lose nothing more."

Sacramozo knows the moment that is auspicious for Andreas's union with Maria. He chooses that moment for voluntary death—he is sure he will return, to be united to Maria transformed, (he knows that elements too are transformed)—that Andreas will then be forced to yield before him—how, he purposely avoids considering—fills him with sorrowful sympathy for Andreas.

He has always known that this would happen to him in his fortieth year. He divides his life thus: three periods of twelve years: the first, fulfilment, revelation; the second, confusion; the third, damnation or ordeal. Then three years of action, then the fortieth—*annus mirabilis*.

"The truly philosophic act is suicide" (Novalis).— Suicide on the one hand as the most sublime act of self-enjoyment, the indisputable dominion of the spirit over the body, on the other as the most sublime communion with the world; harmony in contrast, at last, with the final word of Oriental philosophy (Neo-Platonists on suicide).

How, in the smallest, subtlest detail, the body is to be persuaded—that is the secret and the difficulty. At the same time, attention to and reverence for that which does not return.

"To destroy the principle of contradiction is perhaps the supreme task of higher logic" (Novalis).

"Gradual increase of *inward* responsiveness is thus the chief concern of the artist of immortality" (Novalis).

Conversation with Maria on suicide: "Above all, one must be sure of destroying oneself entirely."— Here Sacramozo smiles.

Sacramozo: "Every morning the sun rises on millions of men, but where among those millions is the one heart that responds to it in pure music like the pillar of Memnon?—I stood with ten thousand on a hill, a pilgrimage, etc.,—but my heart was separated from theirs. When has the morning sun ever *really* illuminated me? Once, perhaps, in that brief dream. But I shall go where a virgin light will meet me on virgin shores."—"Every beginning is serene. Hail to him who can always begin again!"

DAY OF SACRAMOZO'S DEATH.
The preparation. Fasting. Aspect of the world. Onset of doubt. Anxiety, resolve wavers, grows firm again.

Last conversation with Maria: farewell and meeting again: the power of this conversation on her.

The last afternoon, evening. His thoughts *during*. The drops: the realization that he can stop between one drop and the next. Ecstasy of dissolution, how it fades at the thought that he can stop. The aspect of the world between life and death: the finality sanctifies the ecstasy: an enormous *honouring* of God in His creatures: a moving into the temple of God. Onset of fear of death: paroxysm. Transfiguration.

Before death: hears water flowing, desire to conjure up all water he has ever heard flow.

Stages of dissolution: a wonderful drawing near to every being that is borne towards him by a gentle, shining river; the beings rise like swimmers out of a holy stream: he knows that nothing he has done in his life has been in vain. The approaching beings singular, like a kiss dissolving the soul—the blueness of a garment, the breath of a lip, the voice of a bird (the objects in the room: sky-blue stuff, a mask, silver candelabras, flowers, fruit, bowls of water)—he takes it for the promise of an ineffable union, and now knows he cannot turn back.

The death-room of the Knight with alabaster lamps and flowers. His ecstatic letter of farewell: universal love. For him, this is no vague dissolution, but the most sublime preservation of personality.

AT THE same time, Andreas wins Zustina in the lottery. She wants to give herself to him, hoping by that to win him so that he will remain her husband. Confesses the trick by which she made him win, which was very cleverly contrived. Her tears and her recovery: evidence that Nina too is in love with him.—News of Romana.—Zustina speaks of the way in which Nina loves him in contrast to her own, deduces both, very acutely and delicately, from their physical constitution. At this moment, Zustina is extraordinarily beautiful. Zustina: "when Nina is in love, everything stops for her soul: the world has changed—she cannot understand how she can have lived yesterday. Till now I was never in love —and if there is no way of being in love but Nina's, I still don't know love. For the world is always the world for me, even though it contains a being whom it is delicious to meet."

LAST CHAPTER

As Andreas takes flight and travels up the mountains, he feels as if the two halves of his being, which were torn asunder, were reuniting.

At San Vito, he finds a farmhand driving home by night. When he reaches Castle Finazzer the next day, Romana is not there. Bit by bit he hears that she has fled to the alp on his account; then that she has had a terrible fever, has constantly spoken of him, then taken a vow never to see him again unless he comes from Vienna to make her his wife. (Modesty now as infinitely exaggerated as previous freedom).

He leaves a decisive letter for Romana.

Last Chapter. He leaves at daybreak. They arrive at sunrise. Up to the Alps with the mother. Romana creeps into the farthest cranny and, in the end threatens to throw herself down from the precipice.

ANDREAS OR THE UNITED

THE LADY WITH THE SPANIEL

GENERAL PLAN (rough), 12. IX. 1912.
I. Arrival. Lodging. Lottery. Visit to the cocotte. First
meeting. II. The Knight of Malta. Conversation. Visit
to the Countess after another visit to Nina. III.
Developments in the affair with the widow. Amorous
friendship with the Countess. Jealous of the Knight.
IV. The Countess is moved: her story. The widow:
the present in its most fiery form, impish, knowledge
of the "other." V. The Countess begins to withdraw
(change of confessor). Evening visit. The *billet* with the
threat. VI.... VII. Evening visit; feeling in Andreas,
as he goes up, how completely he has changed. The
weight of experience: nothing that could not have
happened.

ANDREAS—Reason for sending him on the tour:
difficult, protracted convalescence after a mental crisis,
some listlessness, loss of a sense of value, confusion
of ideas.

Influence of a Father Aderkast who has suspended life for Andreas, made it illusory (performances of Calderon).—The meeting with Father Aderkast (who bears down on him fulsomely—he feels as if his whole past were breaking in upon him, inescapably) interwoven with an adventure with Mariquita: the more distraught Andreas grows, owing to the repeated meetings with Father Aderkast, whose insistence he can hardly understand, the more charming he appears to Mariquita.

Andreas does not really believe in his experiences; what happens to him, of all people, cannot be worth much: he is always at extremes, on the one hand sensual, on the other idealistic.—He always assumes that people must know what is going on in him.— His demands were gentle, without insistence, he was content with little.

Andreas's apprenticeship: to recognize the existence of higher things, to realize the value of life.

In his memories of childhood, there remains a painful confusion which his whole life will hardly suffice to unravel. To die reconciled to one's childhood. (Journal: "I should like to die reconciled to my childhood.")

His grandfather, a carter at Spitz, came down from the forest. Drives Princess Brunswick who notices him and hires him as a groom in place of one who has fallen ill. The Emperor rides to meet her with a hundred horsemen, has himself presented to her last under the *incognito* of Count Falkenstein, but as he kisses her hand, presses it, so that she jumps up, startled and falls into his arms, and he now kisses both of her hands in turn. (This in 1716, the grandfather born 1699; Andreas's father, born in 1731, is now forty-eight.) The Spanish *genre* in these stories.

CLOSE of the tour chapters: encounter with the "woman on the Aar"—the adventure with the inconsolable widow.

Leaving the Finazzer farm: he does not believe in himself; he creates in himself the figure of another, who will return. Now startled in the house on the river, where the mourning widow comes towards him with her "Really you! It is really you! You cannot escape yourself!"—The mood of supreme exaltation, which has lasted for several days since the moment of the mountain, suddenly reversed in this adventure (the widow's hand on his breast in the night).

A German-speaking widow from the lowest-lying of the *Sette Communi*. The picture of the accident painted on paper, the wedding-ring attached. Sends her sixteen-year-old daughter to kneel and weep by the river. Her cough (hysterically exaggerated by herself)—at times she tells the story in fuller detail. The picture is her prayer-book, her all.—Impression on Andreas: "A single moment!"—from this moment on he can pray, it comes home to him. (In between, the merchant's servant, looking after his luggage, abrupt revulsion from prayer. Idle, empty chatter with a fellow traveller about the gentry of the *terra ferma*)—The widow's complaints and monologues, have not stopped for seventeen years: the daughter's callous way of detailing it all, saying in a weary drawl, "Nothing gives her pleasure, she feels the world as her coffin"—the mother says the same thing, but in a raving way, so that even in her anguish there is still a trace of the breath of God, of the inexhaustibility of nature and life. On the other hand, even the daughter's bearing is dreadful, list-lessly dragging herself along by her mother's side, listlessly answers, "Yes, yes"—with side-long looks, listlessly saying, "Father has been dead for eighteen years now, and she will not stop, she will never get over it till she lies in her grave."—Here Andreas becomes aware of how mysteriousness is the connec-tion that rules between the moment and the year, even between the moment and life as a whole: how in a way a moment can devour a whole life (— something similar in the Countess's fate).

He hears her talking, interrupted by weeping; she

means to drown herself. The daughter hard beyond her years. He begins to feel that the whole of existence rests on a healthy feeling of self-confidence, like Mount Kaf on an emerald. After all these imaginings, he feels inseparably united to Romana—in very truth her spouse.

The scene where the daughter tries to drag her mother away to stop her making herself a nuisance to the stranger, saying to her mother, who is clinging to the stranger's breast, the bitterest, most frigid truths. "That is a strange man. Chance, which he will curse, made him stop here for the night. He cares nothing about what has happened to you, he curses the place and your screams; they pierce his ears. His carriage will hardly have turned the corner when he will have forgotten you and me like the vermin in a dirty inn."—Andreas's feelings terribly torn, confronted by misery—absolutely infinite. He despises himself for every comfort he possesses...—here the journal of the tour breaks off abruptly.

He did not reflect on all these experiences in detail, yet they were all present in him; each one was in some way always there, his soul was like a quivering magnetic needle: all these things perpetually diverted it from its pole; he was empty and overburdened. His nature needed and longed for passion which, by carrying us away, relieves us of the burden of self.

The house on the river, with the inconsolable widow, in all the rooms, outhouses, etc., encompasses him completely.—In her grief-worn face a sudden brightness, the eyes kind, the mouth pretty, the natural in its greatest truth and purity.—Question: whether the existence of his parents is not hell in disguise.

Andreas roaming sadly about: these quite small details: picking up a twig, throwing it away with love, but gently, not far from him, still feels it as it lies there, licks blades of grass for joy.

He has listened to the widow as no one has for a long time past: that is why she comes to him in the night, touches his breast—where, after such a long lapse of time, she feels a human response, something of him she has lost wakes and lives again.

The evening, at supper: she walks up and down, raving of the dead man. The daughter says: "The wind is in the south."—She takes the stranger's hand "Oh take that—only that from me—that I did it of set purpose, with full knowledge. Do I not stand like a stone in the wall? It is on the point of collapsing, that is just why it must stand fast! Can you understand me? The lust of murder (*imp of the perverse*) is nothing compared to it. I did it out of frozen horror of the world"—(at once contradicts herself, accusing herself of devilish selfishness). Frightful pause, in which life, even movement, stands still, transfixed. The daughter pushes her away: "The gentleman's supper is ready, leave him alone!"—how young the mother looks in her moments of greatest anguish.— The daughter: the priest dismisses her from the confessional for obdurate despair.

Andreas: in a generally dull, a dispirited state of mind, certain subtleties, certain improbable, favourite associations, which his mind constantly pursues, which he feels to be reality itself, while he is never aware of the rest of life as unalloyed. He is thus visited by a sense of the actual that evening by the river where the mourning widow's house stands. Then the strange adventure in the night when the half-mad woman kneels on his breast. Previously, he identifies himself with the dead man, imagines that that look came from his eyes. In bed, thinks intensely of Romana.

Later, reversing the roles, he puts himself in the place of the wretched murderess, Romana in the place of the man. He is morbid enough to imagine the murder. All his mania of self-abasement converges on this point: he pictures to himself all that he has destroyed in Romana: he does not let her die completely, but live on, a joyless spirit—by this the richness of her life is just revealed to him—he feels bound to her as never before, the value of life dawns upon him—he is happy.—"By what are we moved—

155

by what power—from what point?" he asks, and he is appalled by his ignorance of the power which is above all things.

Constant elevation of the substance Romana by all that happens. He can only possess Romana when he believes her.

In the widow's house. At the window, at sunrise, clouds over the river. Profoundest experience: the presentiment of all love and no love in himself: the presentiment: Nothing can happen to me. I shall not be a loser in the end. Before, in stages, deepest temptations; his chief fear, to be cheated of the essential, of the substance of life.—To himself: "Whoever you are, religious or irreligious, child or father, you cannot be cast away, something sustains you." He imagines he can comprehend this something. What he did not believe himself worthy of, what he did not believe possible, what he refused to believe himself capable of—in the past it seemed possible, in dreams it was unassailably his.—One thing above all he found toilsome—to attain to himself, and in this toil his nature was fulfilled.

ANDREAS's path: first to become capable of love, then to learn that body and spirit are one. He has suffered all the time from this dualism: now the one, now the other in himself, seemed worthless. Now he learns to feel, one behind the other, to feel the one always sustaining the other.

How Romana comes to life in him: single traits, a smile as of a secret understanding with him. These moments, when she comes to life in him, always bring anxiety, which alternates with serenity. Once he thinks he sees Romana sitting on the Riva on a trunk: she is beginning to unpack. He does not dare to approach her.

Chapter I, end: Andreas sitting on the bed. It is easier for a camel to pass through the eye of a needle than for him to become, in the real sense of the word, the lover of the Spanish woman, of Zustina, or of Nina—anyone else could. Now, thinking of Romana, beautiful radiance: the walk. Four castles in the air in which he lives with each of the four.

Episode of the tailor's wife—at the same time, estrangement from the Knight. The wife of a tailor, who would like to be married to him. The little tailor humours her. Humble surroundings, full of back-stairs gossip, about strangers in the town too. Offers to belong to him and to procure others for him: at the same time, immense respect for virtue. Quite primitive lower-class life, like the life of the people in ancient times. The tailor's wife has sixteen brothers and sisters. Kindly eyes and a pretty mouth, *accommodant*, at the first meeting she treats him like a great gentleman, afterwards more as one of her own class. Her husband dies. The woman's children: the grave boy, as he gazes at him, seeming to forget himself, the girl nestling up to him with a rather deceitful look.

Here Andreas is, in a way, at home: with the Countess he feels as if he were not alive, but only dreaming; he wonders if he has ever lived. This life in the tailor's house, which he mentions to nobody, makes him feel a liar and traitor.—During this time Andreas sits to Zorzi for his portrait, maliciously breaks off the sittings. To frighten him, Zorzi threatens him with intervention by the authorities. The catastrophe caused by the death of the husband, the children change towards him, their bitterness. Andreas reproaches himself: "Can I say that I am bound to anyone?"—He cannot bear the sight of the pictures in the churches, they humiliate him, the figures in them are so manifold. He is disgusted by his own capacity to understand everybody with his mind and his heart—even the spy Zorzi, an old hunchbacked messenger, and so on. He wants to confess this self-contempt to the Knight, but does not do so. The Knight realizes his state, sees in his changed, contemptuous way of speaking that he is at odds with himself.

THE KNIGHT gives Andreas Ariosto to read on account of the wonderful "world" that is his. He does not read Ariosto with an eighteenth-century mind. He understands what the Knight means when he says that there is no such thing as the past: everything that exists is present, more is born at the present moment (feeling when listening to Bach's music).

For Andreas, Fate is fulfilled in what is most individual—in what is most individual lies power. Nothing that is to work, magically is in any way vague or general, but most particular, most momentary. Love—illuminated by a sudden ridiculous fancy, an awkwardness, a hesitation, as well as by a gesture of courage, of freedom. The ordinary "I" an insignificant construction, a scarecrow.

Andreas and the two women: "The nature of things is completely exhausted in opposition and intensification" (Goethe at eighty)—on the one hand, demands more of each every time—to what end? (Tact embodied in the bearing of the Knight)—on the other hand, sense of polarity; in each he loves the other with the most delicate, chaste love, and in this way learns to abandon the search for the absolute in the world.

Andreas fears to become aware, in Maria or Mariquita, of the other being, and hence to lose the unique quality of the loved one. He is on the point of murdering Mariquita in order to save Maria for himself. (The temptations to which his weakness is here exposed—"learn to live!")

Andreas's humble wish to be Mariquita's husband. Gradual realization of the impossibility of the step: imagines letter to his parents announcing the plan.

MARIA AND MARIQUITA.—Novalis: "all evil is isolated and isolating, it is the principle of separation"— by union, separation is abolished and not abolished, but wickedness (evil) as apparent separation and conjunction is actually abolished by true separation and union, which only exist in reciprocity.

Maria	Mariquita
wishes to live to be an old woman	is afraid of growing old
often imagines herself dead (here she coincides with Sacramozo's conquest of time)	dreads death
loves old people	dislikes seeing old people
is afraid of children	draws children to her

MARIA's emotion over an old woman whose skin nobody seeks to touch.

Mariquita is greedy and an artist in cookery.

Maria enjoys good food too, but suppresses this tendency it and knows nothing about cookery. Mariquita's concupiscence of experience, boundless curiosity to set her foot everywhere, to enter every possible situation, to visit every place of ill repute. Everything that Andreas points out (the beauty of flowing water, etc.) she absorbs in intenser form. She hears all the talk of the town, knows where everything is going on, where this or anything is to be seen (the vegetable market towards morning, the fish market, fantastic episodes in cellars, stage-coach drives on the mainland, episode of the tight-rope-walkers).

Mariquita an utterly baffling person, lets herself be kissed, nothing more, hints that she is a respectable woman, but has a lover, of course.—He takes her to casinos, to other places of amusement; sometimes she stiffens convulsively, then suddenly looks at him with the face of Maria.—With the Countess, it seems to him a prodigy, not seriously to be thought of that she might give herself; with Mariquita, an absurdity that she does not. In both he goes too far, both are funnels through which he falls into an abyss. He longs to speak to the Knight about it; instead, he encounters the Duke, who is having a biting-match with the dogs.

Mariquita to Andreas: "I am infatuated with you because you were the first man I saw after I was free. I know there you are nothing very special after all, but I still see you with rapture in my eyes—it's all chance, after all."—"On that day I had really got out for the first time I had already contrived to write letters."—the power to enter into adventures because she is absolutely free.

Mariquita receives visitors in a strange lodging which she alleges to belong to her mistress, and has had lent to her on fraudulent pretexts: she pretends to be a *dame de compagnie* or something of the kind. The conflict in Andreas's mind about marrying her, since he is aware of all her failings, however charming. Her random chatter at times—her dreaminess. "Shall I possess you entirely?" asks Andreas.—"Entirely, and another into the bargain."

How Mariquita makes friends: presents herself as a governess, collecting for religious purposes. Perpetual outings, she has always discovered something. On their excursions, she takes Andreas into all kinds of society, where he has to suffer mockery and scorn, where he is bewildered, imposed on and put to shame: "You would like to become an official?"—Mariquita likes to hear the story of Uncle Leopold.—Among others she takes Andreas to see a lunatic, pretending to be his niece or housekeeper; he comes in, talks to himself without seeing those present.—Once she hits on the idea of enticing him into a strange house for Andreas, then sending him home with the "other" in her confusion and shame. The other does not say a word, seems mortally ashamed and frightened, so that Andreas leaves her.

Her most beautiful moments: her power of perceiving elements of purity even amid apparent ugliness, at the fish market, at the vegetable market, buying provisions for a meal.—He wants to travel to the widow's house with Mariquita; after protracted difficulties the plan falls through. She will never revisit any place they visited together the time before. Thus each time she unravels the web.— Andreas: "If only I knew something about your solitude. What are you like then?"

Mariquita likes to question Andreas about the Knight, it is almost as if she sometimes wavered between the two. "What would he say or do then? Ah, is he like that? Do you admire him very much? Would he like me?"

Mariquita sees the Knight speaking to Maria with loving urgency. She (what resists in her) prevents Maria from really loving the Knight.

Mariquita declares that she knows everything about the Countess, back into the first year of her life: she recounts part of her biography—never her own. Andreas asks, "And what about you when you were a child?"

Mariquita, having once fainted from fright, turns

into Maria—during the adventure in the storm, on the quay, in a strange house to which he has carried her. On that day she was tired, had not had enough sleep: a beautiful sunset, then a thunderstorm.

MARIA's story: abandoned after passionate love, marries a man she does not love, who only possesses her once: he falls very ill: she nurses him in a wayside inn—then the faithless lover comes to her window.—Maria's fundamental idea: the infinite—how it is possible to take one man for another.

Her psychic malady dates from the day on which, nursing her unloved husband after the death of her child, she is unexpectedly confronted with the lover, the faithless one. "Life has rent me asunder, God in Heaven alone can put me together again."

What happened: gradually she brings herself to answer some of the lover's letters, agrees to meet him once. Here, she does not think beyond the delight of the meeting, but into that delight she plunges entirely: it is an utterley different thing for her from seeing him pass by often: for her the meeting is like the plastic compared with the visual—there is something added. In comparison, her husband loses relief more and more. Just before the meeting, she pauses, turns round and goes home. She feels as though her husband were sitting at her embroidery frame, waiting for her, as though his eyes were on her. As she is going home, she feels her lover behind her back, but does not turn round, has the strength to reach the threshold. She goes upstairs, opens the door; her husband is actually sitting at the embroidery frame, his eyes upon her, but he is dead.

In her marriage, temporary loss of sense of value. Sitting alone at her mirror, the Countess once sees how she changes after everything in her mind has taken on a different aspect. The torture in her face struggles with triumph—then Mariquita stands up and steals downstairs.

Once, when Maria is talking to Andreas and the Knight (about Spanish titles and successions, purposely, tediously, because she does not *want* to excite herself), she forgets herself: the other face appears, her tone changes completely, her eyes swim, a burning look meets Andreas—then it is over, she turns deathly pale, has difficulty in picking up the thread. During this glowing moment, Andreas says to himself, "I am possessed, my imagination has called up the other"—he turns red with shame and tears come into his eyes.—Andreas cannot bring himself to assent to the identity of the hands, he insists on finding a difference.

In Maria, subliminal horror of everything happening in the street, increasing reluctance to drive out, which the Knight tries to overcome. Purification, the heart reduced to ashes, glorifies self-mortification, interest in Platonism, tendency to Molinism.

The sermon she has heard in the afternoon about the work of the worms in the human corpse, and at the same time how we are forgotten even by our nearest: how there is no salvation here save with God.

Confessor: Spaniard. Mariquita has a curious relationship to him; she writes to him too, she threatens to lead Maria into another way of life. She resists his look.—Strong desires felt by Mariquita are felt as impulses by Maria.

Mariquita on Maria: she refused to be a real woman—would not forget Christ.

Andreas—Maria: it comes to taking a room: his dread of possessing her—unconscious even to himself.—Maria feels a voice warning her, repeats tonelessly what she imagines the voice said to her: "Do not do it, do not do it."

Her confessions when she is ill (apparently delirious, but she is not delirious)—how Mariquita has cut her feet from her body and hidden them. As she tells this, Andreas rushes from the room. He now receives incessant letters from both. Finally, the lady enters a convent.

THE KNIGHT of Malta.—He moves in a time which is not quite the present, and in a place which is not completely here.—For him, Venice is the fusion of the classical world and the Orient, impossibility, in Venice, of relapsing into the trivial, the unmeaning. Morosin Peloponnesiaco his great-grandfather. Possesses some antiques, among them an early torso.

Several beings in him: when he is gardening, out on the Brenta, in shirt-sleeves, he anticipates the bourgeois of 1840: for Andreas the premonition of how his own grandchildren will live.

Relatedness. Alone with the child, the child looks up: "Out of the substance, which I may not seek—for I am that substance—all the heavens and hells of all religions are constructed—to cast them away would be gross darkness.—The child's look: binds me, the words in my mouth, to these walls, to their protection, to what is simply there."—*Impavidum ferient ruinae*—an interpretation, a consideration of inner powers, a mustering of resources: only the cataclysm reveals supreme ecstasy.

Sacramozo's two dreams at the desk in the magistrate's court at Bruneck: (i) He is living alone at the castle—a cock crows, then a second time; a bell rings. He stands up, barefoot: through the soles of his feet he feels everything, right down into the mountain. The miller's daughter at the gate; lights the fire, waters the cattle in the great hall—purely symbolic ceremonies. Then, in the arbour, he marries her to his son. From the mountain wall opposite there issue silver ancestors, so beautiful that he cries in his dream, "I am dreaming."—(ii) Everything has two meanings: he is governor, but nobody must know it. In the entrance hall, a fire, maids, the prisoner chained to the wall. Denial. The prisoner: "Do you know me, then?" Every time in between, he flies through the landscape: brooks, graveyards—hither, thither. Already weary of his fight, he believes that he must discover who the other is—it is like a mislaid key.—The cock crows. He knows that it is for the third time, and knows that he has betrayed his Saviour.—The real governor comes up to him: "I have the strangest news for you: the Count of Welsberg has returned from the Turkish war"—he was believed to have been captured and beheaded by the Janissaries.

His hypochondria (indescribable dependence on the quality of the air): his pride with regard to these things, reticence.—Antipathy to raucous shouts, barking of dogs.

A man must become devout in the struggle for perfection. His explanation of what has taught him to despise the sensuously perfect—although he is sensitive to it (the sensuous perfection expressed in

168

Veronese in the relation of a perfect white to a bare throat, the same in Correggio)—the dilapidated condition of Venice has taught him the vanity of all things.

Perfectomania: to plan sumptuous festivals ends in the belief that no festival is perfect but the funeral of a Carthusian monk.

His key, that he can see through the motives of others, their nature: just as, for a devout man, everything is over when he realizes that the other is godless, incapable of seeking God; so, for him, everything is over when he feels no disinterested and steady striving upwards: he clings to what he calls the human, he is quick to divine the merely partial.—"What is the use of a confused striving, an isolated good quality? I will have nothing to do with the sieve of the Danaides, the rock of Sisyphus."

Sacramozo's interpretation of the Gospel saying: "Seek ye first the Kingdom of God and all these things shall be added unto you" (here, in created beings, he seeks the Kingdom of God). "The *ergon*," says the Fama, "is the sanctification of the inner man, alchemy is the *parergon*." *Solve et coagula*. The universal binding agent—gluten; his universal solvent—alkahest; in love, both are present. In love, always sublimate, etherealize, sacrifice life, the moment, to the higher, purer thing which is to be distilled from them—seek to fix this higher, purer thing.

The Knight: a motto: *Le plus grand plaisir de tous les plaisirs est de sortir de soi-même*, in *Amours d'Eumène et de Flora* (in von Waldberg, *Geschichte des Romans*). The evil mood that precedes his crises: he is then actually unpleasant, or rather insufferable, even discourteous. The look of contempt for everybody, even for Andreas. His crushing mockery of Andreas: he literally annihilates him (and himself too). The consuming irony and tormenting restlessness that drive him. In this condition, one of his crises coincides with a momentous crisis in Maria: Mariquita suddenly speaks to him, mocks him. He runs away, passes through a crisis of deepest self-abasement, from which he rises to supreme purity and joyful victory. Before this, he hurries to various places (to Nina too) where he suffers rebuffs and humiliations.—"How," he wonders, "can the worthy substance arise from the worthless, the eagle from the chameleon, the jewel from dirt?"

Knight: the complete collapse of the man of forty. He can no longer expect further illumination, redeeming revelations, and cannot imagine that those older than he should have resources that are withheld from him: he can approach nobody with entreaty, in confiding discipleship: what is capable of redemption is his *work* (the young man there before him)—He himself is his own last resort: he no longer looks on life with curiosity, very many relationships are no longer possible. He has realized all this, his morbidity intensifies it: he cannot really reconcile himself to his actual age. With the Countess he is like a schoolboy: that is a task beyond his powers: everything he does to her is a pretence. Appalling doubts at this point: every time they arise, he has the decency to put a stop to them and go on *doing.*— That is the most heroic of all human conditions (see Frederick the Great).

Who could imagine him infinitely weeping, infinitely wooing?—he lacks that touch of the actor which is essential to the priest, the prophet, without which they cannot exist. How every faculty requires for its existence its own opposite latent in it: the unspeakable delight, for the modest, to think that they might overcome their modesty, for the proud, the cold, to imagine themselves glowing.—Thus, in every impulse to take, the profound impulse not to take (the secret in Grillparzer's relationship to Kathi)—duality incorporated in Maria and Mariquita. Sometimes Sacramozo bewilders Andreas with disclosures of this kind, for instance, once after an evening together (supper, casino) when Sacramozo greeted a large number of people.

Sacramozo's way of telling a story.—Instead of "I was once in Japan with pilgrims," he says, "Go to Japan! You will walk three, five days with a band of pilgrims... the question is whether you will see the sun rise in purity..."

Knight: "Note that each of us only becomes aware in the other of what conforms to himself; we create statues round about us in our own dimensions. Problem: in what does union with a human being consist? in understanding, in possession, in first approaching that human being?..." (hint of Indian speculation).

Knight to Andreas: "Does a young man really know what he demands, what he wants?"—"all these connections, and whether they lead to anything— that requires guidance from above."—The Knight possesses the conception of power, which Andreas has yet to acquire.

Knight and Andreas compared: Andreas: Faith in authority ramifying to the uttermost periphery of existence, so that he feels that everything he experiences is analogous to, but not identical with, something *real*, his actions too. The real doers are elsewhere; his inhibitions, his naïveté in face of life, are his own. Knight: doubts not himself but his fate. In suffering, in enjoyment, he had the whole, two-sided, in one, but everything remained partial to him (while Andreas feels that everything remained partial to him, not "the grasp to get it"). Knight knows: my command is a command, my smile has a general power to win—but, *en somme*, what is the good of it?—Knight has not Andreas's wavering, his doubts, his fitfulness—he is sure of results, but it can often happen that he finds himself in a vacuum with them: "*Eh bien*! what now?" says his double. "Aha!—well, well, what now!"

Andreas's dawning realization that there is for the Knight, who can speak to everybody, before whom all barriers fall, *one* barrier all the same. This thought has something of it which moves him almost to tears.

The affair with the letter. Chapter V.—Zorzi: "The Knight has left a letter behind." Andreas: "Let me take it back to him"—almost as if his tongue had said it of himself: the fulfilment of his wish means infinitely much to him. Runs after him. Knight puts it in his pocket, unforgettable hasty gait. Knight returns a few minutes later. "You are mistaken. The letter did not belong to me." Andreas: "And certainly not to me." Chapter VI, a few days later. Knight catches him up. "I must ask you to tell me what could have persuaded you to give me that letter. There are coincidences that leave one no peace. The inside and the outside of the folded letter were in a different hand; I think it belonged to me." He blushes as he speaks; Andreas vows to use the words "beautiful" and "ugly" with caution.

Knight hails a gondola in order to read the letter, begins while the gondolier is getting the gondola ready—forgets to get in. The gondolier does not like to draw his attention. He stands up quickly and pushes the letter into his pocket. Gets in, tries to get over the letter. Mistakes several houses for his own, then feels his own then feels utterly restless at home, wants to burn the letter.—Foreboding of death through the letter.

He believes that one or the other of his two servants has done away with the letter—for what possible reason? the elder to protect him? the younger to injure the elder? At last he finds the letter, reads it over; he finds it among travel notes, where his hand has put it in a kind of somnambulism, at a particular place, next to a particularly significant note on Japan. Deeply and singularly shaken by this slight experience.—His degree of sympathy, and hence his comprehension of his two servants. He cannot possibly disturb the elder, who has relatives visiting him: it occurs to him that that is why he went up the front staircase. He reflects on this himself; his servants in Japan, where he had fourteen of them, men and women, come into his mind. He notices in passing that he is forming within himself a whole chain of thought, always turning on this servant—his old servant: he and the servant always at cross-purposes: the young servant, who is always quarrelling with the elder. The Knight locks up the letter, and at once takes it out again.

After the letter: the Knight tries to bring reason to bear on in his inward tumult, to reduce to order (by Locke's method) the associations unclaimed: he reveals in himself courtesy, grace, modesty. His inexhaustible inward powers—confident—hosts of angels which he summons. A man's whole nature must come to light in such a struggle with inward disorganization: his wanted trains of thought, his favourite associations.—Subtle association with a memory of travel: pilgrimage with Japanese, perception of light. He had resolved to hail every day, the coming of the sun—why can he not always welcome it?—he tries now to marshal the associations towards a higher, purer order; he knows that only inadequacy opposes the Cosmos. He kneels, prays to the supreme being. Chaos and death breathe upon him: on the point of succumbing, he is like the delicate boy he was, with a fleeting colour on his cheeks.

A MEETING BETWEEN ANDREAS and the Knight on a ship at anchor. Invitations from the captain, rather mysterious. Courtesans—one completely veiled

(Mariquita). Sacramozo obviously embarrassed by the veiled woman: he certainly leads the conversation with assurance; he is deeply interested by an Indian, who takes part, but does not eat with them.—Everything has happened at Mariquita's instigation: "I wanted to see you together for once." This is the only time that Sacramozo and Mariquita meet. On the way home, they say nothing about the whole affair, nothing about the invitation. Andreas feels that the Knight believes it was the Countess. Their conversation turns on fate and death. That night, Sacramozo invites Andreas home for the first time.

The masque: a solemn symbolic festival. Andreas's initiation. What costume Sacramozo wore at the masque remains a secret. Echo of Hafiz's relationship to the boy cupbearer, whom he makes happy out of the flames of his love for Suleika.—Culminating point of the masque, a kind of meeting between Maria and Mariquita, or transmutation of Maria, who is brought in in a state of hypnosis: it ends badly.

The idea hovering before the Knight. The greatest magician is he who can work magic on himself. This his goal, since he is threatened by: confusion, the failure to understand those nearest to him, the loss of the world and himself—all this in his relationship to Maria.—At the same time, Maria unwittingly feeds

his knowledge of that other aspect of the world—
Mariquita having taken it on herself to entice the
Knight away from Maria by letting him suspect the
side of Maria that is turned towards Andreas. (She
keeps this game quite hidden from Andreas.) For
Mariquita fears the Knight as Maria's strongest sup-
port in life.

Knight: "In reality, we know only when we know
little; doubt grows with knowledge" (Goethe)—"These
are men who love and seek their like, and there are
others who love and seek their opposite." (Goethe)—
But then are men like the Knight capable of having
a like and an opposite?—That he no longer understands anyone—the less he understands, the more he
feels how Andreas is growing in feeling, intuition
and knowledge—is balanced by the arcanum: he has
found one who will understand, loving. Thus his
withdrawal becomes lovely, as one who passes into
the mirror to be united with his brother. The circle
comes to have profound meaning for him. The pre-
dominance of the circle in the works and notes of
Leonardo.—When the sun is low, we live more in
our shadow than in ourselves.

The allomatic: the meagreness of earthly experience. He is drawn to the Countess because the other
element in her means so much to her—he suspects
that here is a soul far advanced on the way of trans-

formation. What attracts him in Andreas: that he is open to influences from others; the life of others is present in him in the same purity and strength as when a drop of blood, or the breath exhaled by another, is exposed to powerful heat in a glass ball— even so the fates of others in Andreas. Andreas is, like the merchant's son (in the *Tale of the Six-Hundred-and-Seventy-Second Night*), the geometrical locus of the destinies of others. (The *lucerna*, or lamp of life: a ball of alabaster, in which the blood of one far distant shows, as it moves and glows, how things are with him: in misfortune, it swells or gleams, at death it is extinguished, or the vessel bursts.)

Sacramozo and Andreas: how each gradually set the other in his own place: this connected with Andreas's repugnance of the continual recollection of his adventure with Gotthilff. Only he holds the past in horror who, remaining at an inferior stage, assumes that it might have been different. "Was I, when that being kissed me first, just anyone, everything turns stale; if I was singled out (with the anticipation of every hour till death) then all is sublime." Love is the anticipation of the end in the beginning, and therefore the victory over decay, over time, over death—Novalis's note on the mystic powers of self-creation with which we credit women, so that we expect them to love anyone (theme of *Sobreide*, also of

Death and the Fool). Love is the attraction exercised on us by those animate objects with which we are called to operate. To operate means to lead an animate organism to perfection by transformation—in relation with Maria: to find, of oneself, the power to feel, the chain of experience as necessary—of a higher stage of the egocentric.

The Knight no longer hopes to have children by Maria. Andreas might become his "son without a mother."

Sacramozo says of Maria: "The earthly possibility that she might be united with me existed, but not the higher one." For him, Maria is his collaborator by virtue of the purity of her being. The element of union with him—he wishes to unite Andreas with Maria. Now that they shall be a couple—then, Maria reborn with Sacramozo reborn (in whom Andreas will also exist).—He must know the truth, hence he knows Maria's life—but the only thing of value to him is the life-secret of every being. And since life is both on the surface and in the depths, the life-secret can only be grasped by the union of the two.

He may have been mistaken in all he did, his attitude justifies him.—Self-enjoyment, the highest, purest—Sacramozo seeks it: the union with himself, complete identity, harmony of the idea of self with the knowledge of self. He tries to impart this condition to Andreas, who is helped by love. The Countess participates in that condition, though for pathological reasons: every impulse which issues from Mariquita is saturated for Maria with the atmosphere of selfhood elevated to the state of mystery—in the same way, Maria is for Mariquita the only thing worth experiencing (she loves and hates her). Maria's confession of the rapture she feels in merging into the "other," the mere foreboding of that state (the first is a rapture mingled with horror)—that that is for her the life of life; that every sweetness, every anticipation even, of the union with God, threatens to plunge her into it. (Conversation with the Spanish confessor about this, her self-reproaches. She feels responsible for more than herself. The Jesuit sets her mind at rest.)

ad Sacramozo: *Quod petis in te est, ne quaesiveris extra* (That which thou seekest is within thee; seek it not outside)—To be master of our own self would mean to be aware of everything, even the subliminal.

A being of supreme awareness can never feel fear, except in actual danger, because all other forms of fear in all presupposes some element obtruded, not with awareness.

Magician who thinks he moves an invisible limb. What else is this but to feel one's will, to look on and feel oneself as one exercising his will, not in the material world (like Napoleon), but in the spirit.

Sacramozo: "The most sacred relationship is that between the appearance and the essence—and how constantly it is outraged! One might think that God had hidden it among thorns and thistles.—We possess an arsenal of truth which would have power to change the world back into a stellar nebula, but every arcanym is enclosed in an iron matrix—by our inflexibility and our stupidity, our prejudices, our powerlessness to understand the *unique*."

The Knight and the world: to think that everything, everything, is veiled. The veiled image of Saïs stands everywhere. His ardent craving for the purity of all things.

His other aspect, which he alone sees: so childish, so weak, inadequate. Would like to wipe himself out of existence. Feels that Maria puts him to the test, sees through him. Her inhibition—in that he sees his own inadequacy. Loneliness and mingling with men are the same thing.

The antinomy of being and having: for him, in the spiritual world, where the important thing for him is leadership, election, as for Andreas in the human world. His great love for one of the most beautiful women he possessed.

In Sacramozo, more and more the belief that his

fictitious existence (as Sacramozo) prevents the ultimate unfolding of Andreas into the manly lover, of Maria (round whom he sees another element hovering like an aura) into the happy beloved.

Knight: "Kneel?—as one kneels to receive teaching from a master revered like a god—this gesture I shall have died without finding it on my way. Will this youth be he who is capable of kneeling?" (he leads the figure through all the vicissitudes which for him exhaust the content of the world). "And shall I find the way to be he?—Not by circumventing his inadequacy, but by absorbing it into myself?"

On death: "To have to leave the theatre before the curtain has even risen."

Dissolution, striven for, means peace as to one's own being, great or small, limited or the powerful, accepted or rejected, about one's own lifetime and the epochs of time and the symbolic vision of things, and about the poor and needy.

The Knight great in his total defeat—a being struggling for his fate: In Andreas's union with the transformed Maria, he finds all in one, faith, love, fulfilment.

Andreas, beside the bed on which Sacramozo's body lies, must feel that, in a supreme sense, he may have been right.

Andreas: Outcome of tour to Venice: he feels with

horror that he can never return to the narrow life of Vienna, he has grown out of it. But the state he has achieved brings him more distress than joy, it seems to him a state in which nothing is conditioned, nothing made difficult, and by that very fact nothing exists. Everything merely reminds him of things, they are not really there. Everything tastes stale, there is nothing to seek, but because of that nothing can be found.—Question: whether these fragments in the kaleidoscope could discover a new arrangement. Envious recollection of his grandfather's journey down the Danube, his first places, success by health and courage, piety and loyalty, and, with it all, a certain robust selfishness and cunning.

Andreas's return.—He was what he might be, yet never, hardly ever, was.—He sees the sky, small clouds over a forest, sees the beauty, is moved—but without that self-confidence on which the whole world must rest as on an emerald;—with Romana, he says to himself, it might be mine.

AFTERWORD

Andreas was found, unfinished, among Hofmannsthal's papers after his death. It consisted of a finished chapter and a collection of notes in the form of brief dialogues, aphorisms and quotations. The main fragment first appeared in the magazine *Corona* in 1930. Two years later, *Andreas* was published in book form with an afterword by Jacob Wassermann—only to be suppressed by Nazi censure. Thus, *Andreas* was not available in the German speaking world until Herbert Steiner's postwar edition.

Let us briefly retrace what is known of the genesis of the posthumous novel. While in Venice in the summer of 1907, Hofmannsthal wrote the first draft of *The Venetian Travel-Diary of Herr von N (1779)*, followed by a series of notes under the headings "Ven. Diary", "Ven. Adventure" and "Ven. Experience". Hofmannsthal had just read Morton Prince's *The Dissociation of Personality: A study in Abnormal Psychology* (New York 1906), which relates the case of an American female student who suffers from a split personality. From this unusual case he derived the double figure of Maria and Mariquita, also known as "the wunderbare Feundin". At the time Hofmannsthal briefly considered writing the novel in the form of letters. The main fragment—roughly a quarter of the projected length of *Andreas*—was written between February 1912 and August 1913. (The title *Andreas or the United* was chosen later that year.) In 1918, Hofmannsthal described *Andreas* in a letter to his friend Hermann Bahr as a "novel, on a limited scale on the youth and life crisis of a young Austrian travelling to Venice and Tuscany". He thought that three to four years would be needed to complete it. However, *Andreas* was put aside in favour of *Nachspiel 1808*, the story of Austria's uprising against Napoleon.

The finished fragment of *Andreas*, written in 1912–13, tells the story of the young knight's voyage from Rococo Vienna to Venice. But *Andreas* is much more than a mere historical novel, a period piece. As a voyage of spiritual discovery it reaches beyond the specific experience of a vanished age; the hero, at first character-less and passive, encounters conflicting emotions that will ultimately lead to regeneration and love. These emotions are rooted in experience; as such they have the value of symbols without ever becoming intellectual abstractions.

The initial episode takes Andreas to Carinthia, where he falls under the spell of the enchanted landscape. Magically enveloped in the landscape's immortality, Andreas is enfolded in a wonderful vision of beauty; and he wishes he could espouse this timeless world untainted by corrupting forces. It is no coincidence that the encounter with Romana takes place in this region of loving simplicity and purity, for Andreas senses—if only fleetingly—that Romana comes from a region of the soul which is hidden but pure. Andreas understands that the path to love is akin to the feeling of sanctitude.

Following an encounter with the evil Gotthilff (God-help), he escapes to Venice. The adventures of Andreas in Venice form the centre of events in which the hero is split, on the one hand towards the sensual, on the other towards the ideal. These conflicting attitudes of the soul are brought to light in his meeting with the woman alternatively described as Maria or Mariquita, which are only "the two faces of the same person". Maria embodies the highest expression of the individual soul; she personifies love in its purest form, but fears contact with life itself. She lacks the ability to become flesh and blood: to lose herself in the sensual moment. Mariquita, on the other hand, belongs entirely to the world and succeeds in revealing the unique and external in sensual appearances. Hofmannsthal noted in the *Book of Friends*, a collection of aphorisms dating from 1922: "Every new acquaintance takes us apart and brings us back together. It is of utmost importance that we experience regeneration". Torn between the extremes of duration and change, loyalty and betrayal, the physical and spiritual in life, Andreas realizes that he must allow himself to be transformed by both; for in this apparently simple contrast is enclosed the double possibility of the soul's attitude to life: emotions, neither anchored at one extreme or another, but mysteriously drawn to each other.

Ultimately, Andreas is brought back to himself by Sacramozo, the Knight of Malta. Sacramozo, the spiritual teacher, awakens a higher awareness of life in Andreas. But Sacramozo belongs to a world which does not open itself—he embodies a form of denial akin to destruction and isolation. To find a link to humankind, Andreas realizes that he must accept the impure, the fragmented in life. Only then will he succeed in uniting the two faces of life which he has glimpsed through his encounter with the mysterious double figure. He knows that he belongs to Romana; thus, in the last, unfinished chapter, Andreas leaves Venice behind and returns to the Finazzer farm.

The novel as it lies, unfinished, before us, ends with a stream of notes, allusions to various situations, brief dialogues, epigrams and occasional aphorisms. These intuitions, dissolved in movement, are loosely woven into a fragmented fabric. Beyond its fragmentary form, *Andreas* is concerned with much that our world has lost touch with: timeless and ultimate experiences, moments of poetic ecstasy in which the wholeness of existence is perceived. The miraculous familiarity of things is revived; heightened sensations strive towards a kind of identification with nature and all things; language is wonderfully attuned to nature and human experience. Images of landscapes, towns and villages through which the young knight has wandered, sights which have delighted his eyes, everything is visually retained. Here perhaps lies part of the enigma of *Andreas*. Hofmannsthal started the novel around visual elements reminiscent of Stifter's tales—but gradually shifted towards incorporating fragments rooted in personal experience. And perhaps that is why Hofmannsthal's novel was doomed. As he felt an increasing distaste for the spirit of the modern age intertwined with a sense of the tragedy awaiting his beloved Austria—he may have found himself reluctant to give shape to Andreas's spiritual journey.

OLIVIER BERGGRUEN